GLOOSCAP AND HIS MAGIC

Legends of the Wabanaki Indians

Canadian Favourites

Glooscap and His Magic

Legends of the Wabanaki Indians

Kay Hill

Illustrations by Robert Frankenberg

McClelland and Stewart Limited

0-7710-4417-9

Printed and bound in Canada

To Marj

Foreword

THESE STORIES, so far as we know, were first told in the wigwams of the Wabanaki Indians, long before the White Man came to North America. Later, white men learned them from the Indian, translating and preserving them in book form. In August, 1960, I was invited to adapt the published Legends to a new art form, that of television, for a program called "Indian Legends," conceived and produced by Mr. Sandy Lumsden of CBHT, Halifax, Nova Scotia. Miss Kathleen Currie, Chief Librarian of the Children's Department of the Halifax Memorial Library, dressed in Indian costume, appeared before the cameras and related the stories, with graphics and background music and sound. The program was repeated across Canada and in parts of the United States during the next two years. Finally, in this present volume, the Legends return to something of their original form—a collection of short stories.

I have, therefore, many people to thank for the eventual appearance of this book. To Mrs. Joe Ann Daly of Dodd, Mead & Company, my editorial advisor; to Robert Frankenberg, the illustrator; to Sandy, Kathleen, the musician and artists and technicians of CBC; to Indian scholars like the Rev. Silas T. Rand and Charles

Leland, and the Libraries who saved the stories from oblivion; and last, but certainly not least, to the Indians—I say, thank you.

The Wabanaki (or Abenaki as later the French called them), meaning "those who live nearest the rising sun," were migratory tribes of the Eastern Woodlands, speaking dialects of the Algonquin language. They included the Micmacs and Malicetes of the Maritime Provinces of Canada, the Passamaquoddy and Penobscot tribes of Maine and Massachusetts, and possibly others. Often hostile to one another, at other times uniting against a common foe, they at all times shared the traditions of a grand mythology, the central of which was the hero, demigod, and trickster—Glooscap.

Leland notes the curious resemblance between these old legends and the Norse myths, which seems to suggest that they may have evolved from the same original source. Both are handled in a bold, artistic manner, with the same genial humor. The Odin of the Norse, like Glooscap, is always a gentleman—benevolent and powerful, yet full of earthy humor. The Loki of the Norse, like Lox the Indian Devil, combines the crudity of Punch with the subtle malevolence of Satan. The stories themselves show a likeness to both Norse and European fairy tales. For example, there is a variant of the Norse story of "The Giant Who Had No Heart in His Body" in the Wabanaki tale of "The Boy Who Worried Tomorrow," and there is an Indian version of "Cinderella" in the story called "Oochigeas and the Invisible Boy."

"Around Glooscap," says Leland, "who is by far the grandest and most sophisticated character ever evolved from a savage mind, there are gathered strange and wonderful beings—cannibal giants of ice and stone, booöins, witches and wizards, fun-loving Ableegumooch the rabbit and Keoonik the otter, the mischievous Badger, and the Megumoowesoos, or Little People."

Much of the original material meticulously recorded by Rand and Leland was found to be unsuitable for an audience of children. Although generally moral in tone, the Legends contained a great deal of religious symbolism, meaningful only to the Indian, as well as some savage and erotic elements. They were inclined to wander down byways in the course of which the characters changed disconcertingly not only from good to evil, but from human to animal. Children today are accustomed to the Aristotelian concept of a unified story with a beginning, middle, and end. It therefore seemed necessary to tighten plots, develop characterization, and invent incidents to explain motivation. In doing this, I merely followed the example of the Indian storytellers themselves who, in passing on the songs and poems of the Old Time, departed in a large degree from the original poetry, omitting some incidents and adding others as memory served.

This book therefore differs from other collections of Indian tales in that it does not attempt to record every incident of Glooscap's mythical career in the scholarly manner, but to present unified and romantic dreams while endeavoring to retain the spirit and flavor of the original. In general, the supernatural heroes of the North American Indian appear as tricksters with contradictory qualities of wisdom and stupidity, of goodness and malice. Only Glooscap of the Wabanaki appears continually as benefactor and friend. Perhaps for this reason, the Legends of the Wabanaki are in spirit and meaning unlike anything else in the mythology of North America.

KAY HILL

Halifax, Nova Scotia

Contents

Glossary

THE Algonquin speech, with its long vowels and soft consonants, is said to be the most musical of all Indian tongues. However, the Wabanaki tribes spoke different dialects of this language, and so a choice had to be made. Because many of the tales are drawn from Rand's *Legends of the Micmacs* and also because a Micmac dictionary was the only one available to the writer, most of the Indian words, though not all, are of Micmac origin. Where spelling has been especially difficult, we have simplified it. Pronunciation is shown phonetically, with the accent indicated and the syllables separated by hyphens.

PRONUNCIATION	IDENTIFICATION
Abistanaooch — A-bis-ta-nay′-ooch	the Marten
Abit — A′-bit	Indian girl, sister of Oochigeas
Ableegumooch — Ab-lee ga-mooch′	the Rabbit
Abukcheech — A-book′-cheech	the Mouse
Antawaas — An-ta-way′-ays	the Woodpeckers
atookwakun — a-too-kway′-kun	wonder tale
booöin — boo-oh′-in	an Indian wizard
Bootup — Boo-tup′	the Whale
Chebec — She-bek′	an Indian youth
cheegumakun — she-ga-ma′-kun	a drum made of bark
Chenoo — She-noo′	a giant-sized wizard; a cannibal giant

GLOSSARY

Coolpujot	Cool′-pu-jo	Giant of Seasons whose name means "rolled over by hand-spikes"
Culloo	Cull-oo′	a monster bird into which certain wizards could transform themselves
Etamankiaks	Et-a-man-kee′-aks	a tribe of hostile Indians
Kakakooch	Ka-ka′-kooch	the Crow
Kaloosit	Ka-loo′-sit	a pretty Indian girl
Kayak	Kay′-ak	an Indian youth
Kedgemakoogee	Ked-gee-ma-koo′-gee	a lake
Keoonik	Kee-oo-nik′	the Otter
kespeadooksit	kes-pee-ay-dook′-sit	the story ends
Kitpou	Kit′-poo	the Eagle
Koondao	Koon-day′-o	a booöin, or Indian wizard who could change himself to a stone or rock
Kwah-ee	Kwah′-ee	hello; hail; Indian greeting
Lusifee	Loo′-cee-fee	the Wild Cat
Magooch	Ma-gooch′	an Indian chief
Magwis	Mag-wees′	an Indian brave
Mahia	Ma-hee′-a	an Indian maiden
Masusi	Ma-soo′-see	favorite daughter of Nokum
Mechipchamooech	Mee-kep-cha-moo′-ek	the Bumble Bee
Megumoowesoos	Mee-gum-a-wee′-soos	fairies, or Little People

Mikcheech — Mik-cheech′	a Micmac Indian
Miko — Mee′-ko	the Squirrel
Mooin — Moo′-in	the Bear
Mooinskw — Moo′-in-squaw	the she-bear
Nokome — No-ko′-mee	an Indian youth
Nokum — No′-kum	father of Masusi
Noogumee — Noo-ga-mee′	grandmother, a term of respect for any elderly female; also Glooscap's house-keeper
Oochigeas — O-she-gay′-as	an Indian girl, sister to Abit and Oona
Oona — Oo′-na	sister of Oochigeas
Seboosis — See-boo′-sis	daughter of Ma-gooch
Sigo — See′-go	a young Indian boy
Tabulech — Ta-bal′-ek	an Indian youth
Team — Tee-am′	the Moose
Teetees — Tee-tees′	the Blue Jay
teomul — tee-oh′-mul	an Indian charm, or totem
tokhonon — tok-ho′-non	an Indian game that became lacrosse
Toobe — Too′-bee	a lazy Indian youth
Tumgwoligunech — Tum-gwo-lee-goo-nek′	the Crane
Uktamkoo — Uk′-tam-koo	Newfoundland
Uskool — Us′-kool	the Fisher
Uskoos — Us-koos′	the Weasel
Widjek — Wid′-jek	an Indian youth
Winpe — Win′-pee	a wizard ruling over the North Sea
Wokwes — Wok′-wees	the Fox

Glooscap and His People

In the Old Time, long before the White Man came, the Indians believed that every rock and river, every tree and bird and animal, possessed a spirit—and some spirits were good and some were evil. Around these spirits, which they pictured as giants and wizards and magical animals, the Indians invented marvelous stories called "atookwakuns," or wonder tales. They tell these stories to amuse the children, even to this day, and the stories the children love best are the stories of Glooscap and his People.

In the beginning, the Indians tell the children, there was just the forest and the sea—no people and no animals. Then Glooscap came. Where this wondrous giant was born and when, they cannot tell, but he came from somewhere in the Sky with Malsum his twin brother to the part of North

America nearest the rising sun. There, anchoring his canoe, he turned it into a granite island covered with spruce and pine. He called the island Uktamkoo, the land we know today as Newfoundland. This, in the beginning, was Glooscap's lodge.

The Great Chief looked and lived like an ordinary Indian except that he was twice as tall and twice as strong, and possessed great magic. He was never sick, never married, never grew old, and never died. He had a magic belt which gave him great power, and he used this power only for good. Malsum, his brother, also great of stature, had the head of a wolf and the body of an Indian. He knew magic too, but he used his power for evil.

It was the warm time when Glooscap came. As he set about his work, the air was fragrant with balsam and the tang of the sea. First, out of the rocks, he made the Little People—the fairies, or Megumoowesoos, small hairy creatures who dwelt among the rocks and made wonderful music on the flute, such music that all who heard it were bewitched. From amongst them, Glooscap chose a servant, Marten, who was like a younger brother to him.

Next Glooscap made men. Taking up his great bow, he shot arrows into the trunks of ash trees. Out of the trees stepped men and women. They were a strong and graceful people with light brown skins and shining black hair, and Glooscap called them the Wabanaki, which means "those who live where the day breaks." In time, the Wabanaki left Uktamkoo and divided into separate tribes and are today a part of the great Algonquin nation—but in the old days only the Micmacs, Malicetes, Penobscots and Passamaquoddies, living in the eastern woodlands of Canada and the United States, were Glooscap's People.

Gazing upon his handiwork, Glooscap was pleased and his shout of triumph made the tall pines bend like grass.

He told the people he was their Great Chief and would rule them with love and justice. He taught them how to build birchbark wigwams and canoes, how to make weirs for catching fish, and how to identify plants useful in medicine. He taught them the names of all the Stars, who were his brothers.

Then, from among them, he chose an elderly woman whom he called Noogumee, or grandmother, which is a term of respect amongst Indians for any elderly female. Noogumee was the Great Chief's housekeeper all her days.

Now, finally, out of rocks and clay, Glooscap made the animals—Miko the Squirrel, Team the Moose, Mooin the Bear, and many, many others. Malsum looked on enviously, thinking he too should have had a hand in creation, but he had not been given that power. However, he whispered an evil charm, and the remainder of the clay in Glooscap's hands twisted and fell to the ground in the form of a strange animal—not beaver, not badger, not wolverine, but something of all three, and capable of taking any of these forms he chose.

"His name is Lox!" said Malsum triumphantly.

"So be it," said Glooscap. "Let Lox live amongst us in peace, so long as he remains a friend." Yet he resolved to watch Lox closely, for he could read the heart and knew that Lox had Malsum's evil in him.

Now Glooscap had made the animals all very large, most of them larger and stronger than man. Lox, the trouble-maker, at once saw his chance to make mischief.

He went in his wolverine body to Team the Moose and admired his fine antlers, which reached up to the top of the tallest pine tree. "If you should ever meet a man," said Lox, "you could toss him on your horns up to the top of the world."

Now Team, who was just a little bit stupid, went at once to Glooscap and said, "Please, Master, give me a man, so I can toss him on my horns up to the top of the world!"

"I should say not!" cried Glooscap, touching Team with his hand—and the moose was suddenly the size he is today.

Then Lox went in his badger form to the squirrel and said, "With that magnificent tail of yours, Miko, you could smash down every lodge in the village."

"So I could," said Miko proudly, and with his great tail he swept the nearest wigwam right off the ground. But the Great Chief was near. He caught Miko up in his hand and stroked the squirrel's back until he was as small as he is today.

"From now on," said his Master, "you will live in trees and keep your tail where it belongs." And since that time

Miko the Squirrel has carried his bushy tail on his back.

Next, the rascally Lox put on his beaver shape and went to Mooin the Bear, who was hardly any bigger than he is today, but had a much larger throat.

"Mooin," said Lox slyly, "supposing you met a man, what would you do to him?" The bear scratched his head thoughtfully. "Eat him," he said at last, with a grin. "Yes, that's what I'd do—I'd swallow him whole!" And having said this, Mooin felt his throat begin to shrink.

"From now on," said Glooscap sternly, "you may swallow only very small creatures." And today the bear, big as he is, eats only small animals, fish and wild berries.

Now the Great Chief was greatly annoyed at the way his animals were behaving, and wondered if he ought to have made them. He summoned them all and gave them a solemn warning:

"I have made you man's equal, but you wish to be his master. Take care—or he may become yours!"

This did not worry the troublemaker Lox, who only resolved to be more cunning in the future. He knew very well that Malsum was jealous of Glooscap and wished to be lord of the Indians himself. He also knew that both brothers had magic powers and that neither could be killed except in one certain way. What that way was, each kept secret—from all but the Stars, whom they trusted. Each sometimes talked in the starlight to the people of the Sky.

"Little does Malsum know," said Glooscap to the Stars, "that I can never be killed except by the blow of a flowering rush." And not far off, Malsum boasted to those same Stars —"I am quite safe from Glooscap's power. I can do anything I like, for nothing can harm me but the roots of a flowering fern."

Now, alas, Lox was hidden close by and overheard both secrets. Seeing how he might turn this to his own advantage, he went to Malsum and said with a knowing smile, "What will you give me, Malsum, if I tell you Glooscap's secret?"

"Anything you like," cried Malsum. "Quick—tell me!"

"Nothing can hurt Glooscap save a flowering rush," said the traitor. "Now give me a pair of wings, like the pigeon, so I can fly."

But Malsum laughed.

"What need has a beaver of wings?" And kicking the troublemaker aside, he sped to find a flowering rush. Lox picked himself up furiously and hurried to Glooscap.

"Master!" he cried, "Malsum knows your secret and is about to kill you. If you would save yourself, know that only a fern root can destroy him!"

Glooscap snatched up the nearest fern, root and all, just in time—for his evil brother was upon him, shouting his war cry. And all the animals, who were angry at Glooscap for reducing their size and power, cheered Malsum; but the Indians were afraid for their Master.

Glooscap braced his feet against a cliff, and Malsum paused. For a moment, the two crouched face to face, waiting for the moment to strike. Then the wolf-like Malsum lunged at Glooscap's head. Twisting his body aside, the

Great Chief flung his weapon. It went swift to its target, and Malsum leapt back—too late. The fern root pierced his envious heart, and he died.

Now the Indians rejoiced, and the animals crept sullenly away. Only Lox came to Glooscap, impudently.

"I'll have my reward now, Master," he said, "a pair of wings, like the pigeon's."

"Faithless creature!" Glooscap thundered, knowing full well who had betrayed him, "*I* made no such bargain. Begone!" And he hurled stone after stone at the fleeing Lox. Where the stones fell—in Minas Basin—they turned into islands and are there still. And the banished Lox roams the world to this day, appealing to the evil in men's hearts and making trouble wherever he goes.

Now Glooscap called his people around him and said, "I made the animals to be man's friends, but they have acted with selfishness and treachery. Hereafter, they shall be your servants and provide you with food and clothing."

Then he showed the men how to make bows and arrows and stone-tipped spears, and how to use them. He also showed the women how to scrape hides and turn them into clothing.

"Now you have power over even the largest wild creatures," he said. "Yet I charge you to use this power gently. If you take more game than you need for food and clothing, or kill for the pleasure of killing, then you will be visited by a pitiless giant named Famine, and when he comes among men, they suffer hunger and die."

The Indians readily promised to obey Glooscap in this, as in all things. But now, to their dismay, they saw Marten launch the Master's canoe and Noogumee entering it with Glooscap's household goods. Glooscap was leaving them!

"I must dwell now in a separate place," said the Great Chief, "so that you, my people, will learn to stand alone, and become brave and resourceful. Nevertheless, I shall never be far from you, and whoever seeks me diligently in time of trouble will find me."

Then, waving farewell to his sorrowful Wabanaki, Glooscap set off for the mainland. Rounding the southern tip of what is now Nova Scotia, the Great Chief paddled up the Bay of Fundy. In the distance, where the Bay narrows and the great tides of Fundy rush into Minas Basin, Glooscap saw a long purple headland, like a moose swimming, with clouds for antlers, and headed his canoe in that direction. Landing, he gazed at the slope of red sandstone, with its groves of green trees at the summit, and admired the amethysts encircling its base like a string of purple beads.

"Here I shall build my lodge," said Glooscap, and he named the place Blomidon.

Now Glooscap dwelt on Blomidon a very long time, and during that time did many wonderful things for his People. Of these things you will hear in the pages to follow.

But for the present, kespeadooksit, which means "the story ends."

How Glooscap Found Summer

ONCE, IN THE land of the Wabanaki, it was winter all the time, with dark windy days and bitter nights and never a glimpse of the sun at all. It was a terrible time for the Indians, and for a while Glooscap was at his wits' end to know what to do.

You have heard how Glooscap came to earth from Skyland, how he defeated his wicked brother Malsum, and how he made the Indians and animals. Now when he did all this, the land was warm and pleasant, with trees in leaf and sunlight sparkling on the running streams.

Then, soon after Glooscap departed for Blomidon, suddenly almost overnight, all was changed. It grew cold. The sun disappeared behind the clouds and snow fell from the darkened sky. The lakes grew stiff with ice, and in all the land there was not a flower nor a leaf to be seen. The snow kept the Indians from their hunting grounds, and soon they became weak and ill from hunger and cold. Their Great Chief, Glooscap, seeing all this from his lodge on Blomidon, knew at once that the cold was caused by a giant wizard named Winter, the Ice King. Knowing too that if the cold continued all his people would die, and loving besides to pit his strength against other giants, Glooscap strapped on his giant snowshoes and set out eagerly to find the Ice King.

Deep in the forest, Glooscap came to Winter's wigwam and saw the giant himself leaning in the doorway. The Ice King stood as tall as Glooscap, with long white hair and beard, and a cloak of hoarfrost edged with icicles.

"Winter, you ruffian!" thundered Glooscap, "Lift your icy hand from my people, or I shall drive you away!"

The Ice King laughed.

"We shall see, my brother. Come into my lodge and we will talk the matter over." And he showed Glooscap to the back of the wigwam, which is a place of honor for guests.

When Glooscap was seated, Winter gave him a pipe and began to tell stories. Now Glooscap loved stories, and could not help listening, thinking there was plenty of time to come to the main business. But the Ice King was playing a trick on him. All the while he told his marvelous tales, his servants Frost and Slumber were throwing a charm on Glooscap. The Great Chief began to feel very drowsy. His head felt heavy and his eyelids began to close. Aware at last of his

danger, he tried to rise, but his limbs failed him. Suddenly he was fast asleep. Then Winter went away, exulting, to make the world colder than ever.

Glooscap slept for six months, but at last the charm fled, and he awoke. Angry that Winter had tricked him, he hurried to the lodge of a brother giant called Coolpujot and asked for his help in driving Winter away. Coolpujot was a very huge, very fat old man with no bones, not able to move by himself, but he had certain magic powers.

"I might make the world warm," he told the Great Chief, "but only for a little while. Afterwards, the Ice King's power would be greater than ever, and I should not be able to prevail against him again."

"Work the charm anyway," said Glooscap, for he knew that many of his people were already dead and others dying.

But the fat old giant sighed.

"I can only make the charm work by turning over, and you know I cannot move." So Glooscap called his servant Marten and together, with the aid of handspikes, they rolled the giant over on his other side. Suddenly the sun came out and it was warm again.

"Is there no way Winter can be permanently defeated?" demanded Glooscap.

"There is only one way," said Coolpujot hesitantly.

"Tell me!"

"Far to the south there lives a queen called Summer, who is said to be as strong as Winter, and of whom the Ice King is much afraid. But she may be hard to find."

"I'll find her!" cried Glooscap.

"And perhaps she will not come."

"She'll come!" said Glooscap firmly.

Now it was a very long way to the Southland and Glooscap knew he must get there and back quickly if he were to save the rest of his people. Winter's power would return in a few short months and never go away again.

Glooscap hurried to the edge of the land and sang the magic song which called Bootup the Whale from the ocean.

"What is your will, Master?" asked Bootup, who was one of Glooscap's most faithful servants.

"Take me to the Southland," replied Glooscap, "as quickly as possible." And leaping on Bootup's back, away he went over the waves at a tremendous speed.

The great whale swam and swam and swam, and each day the water grew warmer, and the air, blowing off sunny shores, smelled of spice and flowers. Soon the water became shallow and, in the sand below, the clams called out a warning, "Oh, Whale, keep out to sea, for the water here is shallow and you will go aground."

But Bootup did not understand the language of the clams, and when he asked Glooscap what they said, the Chief answered with a song:

> "They tell you to hurry
> To hurry, hurry along
> Over the water
> As fast as you can!"

Then the whale went like lightning until, all at once, with a terrible shudder, he struck hard and fast in the sand.

"Alas, alas!" wailed Bootup, "you have been my death!

I can never leave the land. I shall swim in the sea no more!" And big tears streamed down his face.

"Have no fear, my friend," sang Glooscap cheerfully. "You shall not suffer. You *shall* swim in the sea once more," and, being now on shore, he placed his bow against the whale's side and with a tremendous push, sent old Bootup off again into deep water. Then he tossed the happy whale his second-best pipe and a bag of Indian tobacco as a reward. Bootup, very pleased, lighted the pipe and, smoking it, swam away to sea. And that is why, to this day, when you see a whale spout, you may say, "There! See? Bootup is smoking his pipe!"

Glooscap now traveled on foot, the sun warm on his face, the forest green and leafy overhead, until he came to a grove of orange blossom where many fair maidens were dancing. In their midst danced one fairer than all the rest, a smiling maid with long golden hair and a crown of flowers, and Glooscap knew at once it was the Queen of Summer. Hiding a little way off, he touched his magic belt and began to sing a song so sweet and tender it made Summer turn her head and move away from her friends.

"Come back!" they cried, but Summer did not heed them. She heard only the voice of Glooscap and ran to him in the forest.

"Come with me to the Northland," said Glooscap. "Help me defeat the giant, Winter."

"I will come," said Summer, "but only for a while, for

this land will be sad and cold without me. How shall I find my way back?"

Now Glooscap knew that with Summer beside him, they could travel swiftly through the forest and would not need Bootup. He took a large moosehide and cut it round and round into a single long cord.

"We will let this run out behind us," he said. "Then, by winding it up again, you will be able to find your way back."

As they ran through the forest, the snow melted before them and the ice disappeared, and soon they came to Glooscap's own land. But here the cold was stubborn and Summer's magic failed, for Coolpujot's charm had run out and Winter's power was great in his own land.

"We must meet Winter and defeat him in his own lodge!" cried Glooscap and, putting her behind him, he strode up to the Ice King's wigwam and called out the Indian greeting in a loud voice:

"Kwah-ee!"

Winter's servants Frost and Slumber saw Summer as she passed, and they fled, but to the Ice King, as he came to meet Glooscap, she was invisible.

Eager to defeat Glooscap again, Winter cordially invited him to enter his lodge, but no sooner were they seated than the Ice King noticed something strange. His cloak of frost was melting! He called out for his servants Frost and Slumber, but there was no reply. He heard water begin to trickle down the rocks in a thousand brooks. He heard a bird sing! He heard buds whispering and laughing as they pushed their way through the bark of a million tree branches. He jumped to his feet in dismay.

"What magic is this?" he cried, feeling his crown of ice drip down his cheeks and his spear shrink in his hand.

Glooscap, with a triumphant smile, stood aside and showed him Summer.

Then Winter knew his power was gone, and he wept.

Summer, who was kind, felt sorry for him.

"We do not want the old man to die," said she to Glooscap. "Is there no way to save him without danger to your people?"

The Great Chief nodded.

"There is a way—a way that will be good for my people too, for too much ease and pleasure leads to laziness." Then he turned to the Ice King and said, "Winter, you will move your lodge at once to the Far North and rule there all year without interruption. At the end of Autumn, when Coolpujot is rolled over, you may come back here and stay six months."

"Hurrah!" cried the giant.

"But at the end of six months," Glooscap went on, "Coolpujot will roll over again and Summer will come from her home in the south, to bring my people the warmth and joy that only she can bring."

And, ever since then, Coolpujot is rolled over with handspikes each Spring and Fall by Glooscap's order, so that the giant Winter and the lovely Queen of Summer may rule the Wabanaki country in turn, between them.

Kespeadooksit—the story ends.

Nokome and the Ice King

Now, WHILE Glooscap was engaged in his struggle with Winter, his People were having a sad and bewildering time.

In the summer that Glooscap left them, the Wabanaki were happy. The running brooks were brimful of fish, and the meadows sweet with berries. Game of all kind abounded in the forest, and as long as the birds sang in the thickets—as long as the streams laughed and glistened and the soft air was fragrant with flowers—the Indians' days were merry and long.

But when the days grew shorter and the red leaves of the maples became brittle and dropped from their branches, the Wabanaki began to be afraid. What was happening to their lovely land? The air had grown chill. The bark walls of their wigwams let in great drafts, and their handsome clothing of scraped and decorated doeskin no longer kept them warm.

The ground grew hard and a white mist began to fall. It sifted through the open places in their lodges and made all damp and dismal. The Indians had never seen snow before, and it frightened them. Who had made it? Where had it come from? Some thought it a spell thrown upon the land by an evil giant, and of course they were right. At that very moment, though they did not know it, their Great Chief was setting out to challenge the Ice King, Winter.

Greater still was the Wabanaki's dismay when ice stilled the brooks and rivers, and the fish were lost to them under the ice. The earth became sick and famished with cold, as deeper and deeper fell the snow, and thicker and thicker froze the river. The Wabanaki hunters crept out of their half-buried homes each morning to hunt for food, but in the white silence they found little or no game, and the least effort exhausted them. Weak from hunger and numbed by cold, many fell and lay silent in the snow. And all this bitter time Glooscap, under Winter's magic spell, lay sleeping and could not help them.

But at last the Great Chief awoke and summoned Coolpujot, who made the sun to shine again and the snow to melt. Alas, however, by now only a few of the Indian families were still alive. In one of these was a youth named Nokome, stronger and more resourceful than the rest. Late in the months of cold he had thought to fasten branches on his feet so he could walk on top of the snow, and in this way, wearing the first snowshoes, he had been able to snare sufficient game to keep himself and his neighbors from starving.

Warmed and heartened by the sun, Nokome watched gladly as the snow melted from the hills and the ice from the river, and all floated down with a gush of laughing water—all except one huge ice cake near the shore. This lodged in a crook of the river and refused to melt, making the air cold all around it. Nokome decided to be rid of it.

Arming himself with a heavy pole, he boldly attacked the monster ice cake. As he pounded away, he sang merrily, "Come on, villain, do your worst. Freeze me if you can!"

At every blow, the enemy gave way a little, until finally it tumbled over on its back and was borne away by the current. As it slid downstream, Nokome heard a loud harsh cry.

"Who dares defy the Ice King? Woe to him who tries Winter's strength!"

Nokome was startled at first, but called back stoutly, "Away with you, Winter, and never come back!"

"I shall come back, never fear!" the voice roared. "Coolpujot's charm will not last long, and then we will discover who is Master!"

As the ice cake slipped out of sight, Nokome laughed, and soon forgot the Ice King's warning, thinking the fine warm days would last forever. But he was wrong. In time, as Coolpujot's charm lost its power, the earth grew cold again. Once more the snow fell and the Indians shivered and grew hungry. Nokome and the other hunters had all they could do to keep alive, and even so a few of them perished before Glooscap found Summer and the warm days came again.

Nokome saw that something must be done. Each time the Ice King came, more people died. In time, if this continued, all the Wabanaki would perish. Nokome would have braved anything to keep Winter away for good, but what could an ordinary mortal do against a giant?

Then, suddenly, it came to him what he must do. Had not Glooscap, their Great Chief, told them that whenever his People sought him diligently in time of trouble, he would help them? Why had he not thought of this before? He, Nokome, would seek out Glooscap and ask him to destroy Winter!

Now this was a very brave thing for Nokome to decide, for no Indian had seen Glooscap since the early days of summer, or knew exactly where he lived. However, the Indians in their fishing expeditions had traveled as far as the mainland and were acquainted with the lobster-shaped peninsula we now call Nova Scotia. Glooscap's canoe had been seen once in Minas Basin, on the far side of that peninsula, and it was rumored that the Master lived somewhere near the green and red mountain of Blomidon.

So, one day, as the red leaves fluttered from the trees,

Nokome set out alone in his canoe, crossing the strip of sea which separated Uktamkoo from the mainland, and entered the mouth of a river. He followed this river to its source, a lake in the South Mountain. After crossing this lake, he lifted his canoe from the water and carried it on his back to a second lake which he also crossed—and so on, from lake to lake in this way, until he came to a stream which led directly down into Minas Basin. Now, far across the Bay, he saw Blomidon, purple in the mist of distance.

It was a long voyage across the Bay, but at last Nokome ran his canoe ashore on Blomidon's beach and gazed up at the red sandstone cliff studded with evergreens and purple stones. He felt suddenly very sure that Glooscap was somewhere near at hand. He would climb the mountain and from its summit be able to see all the territory for miles around. Thus he would discover where Glooscap had his lodge.

Nokome began climbing. The red stone was slippery and he slid back time and again. Ground juniper scratched his face and scraped his hands, but he struggled on. Up and up, until at last he reached the top. Tired and dirty, and gasping for breath, he fell face down upon the grass.

"Kwah-ee!"

The Indian word of greeting echoed in the still air, and Nokome felt a giant hand help him to his feet. There before him stood the immense figure of Glooscap, with beyond him a great wigwam set in the midst of birch trees and guarded by two huge dogs, one black and one white. Nokome had found Glooscap's lodge.

"O Great Chief," cried Nokome, "kill the giant, Winter, or he will destroy us all!" But Glooscap shook his head.

"I have promised Winter he may rule for six months," he said. "Be thankful you have Summer the rest of the year."

"But, Master," Nokome stammered sadly, "even in six months the Ice King can kill many people."

"True," said the lord of men and beasts. "But if you do as I say, you will find you have the power yourself to defeat Winter."

Nokome begged eagerly to be told what to do, but even as Glooscap spoke, his heart sank. He had expected to receive a magician's power, but instead the Great Chief spoke of gathering sunflowers and cutting wood. When at last he ceased speaking, Nokome thanked Glooscap, hiding his disappointment as well as he could, and departed. He paddled wearily back across the lonely miles, convinced his journey had been in vain. Glooscap had put him off with empty words.

Arriving home at last, he saw with alarm that already the dry leaves lay thick on the ground, and he had noticed that whenever the leaves fell, Winter came soon afterwards. He must try the remedy Glooscap had suggested, for he could think of nothing else. Springing ashore, he called the people and told them what to do.

Listening to his words and following his example, the Indians covered their bark wigwams with skins of fur, then laid heavy spruce boughs at the cracks and edges. They cut down all the driest trees, split them into slender sticks, and stored the wood in their lodges. Then they made themselves new clothes, not scraping the fur from the hide as they had always done before. The clothes were ugly and bulky, but warm.

Then the children were set to picking fruits and berries, and the women to cutting up meat, and while the meat smoked over the fire, Nokome taught the women how to make snowshoes of ash splints fastened together with thongs of rawhide. Then the dried meat and fruits were stored in the lodges with the wood. Last of all, Nokome squeezed oil from sunflower seeds and stored the oil in a basket lined with hardened clay.

Now at last, if Glooscap spoke the truth, they were ready for the Ice King, and only just in time. For all through the forest the giant's breath could be felt, stiffening the water in the brooks and coating the ground with frost. The cold air stung the Indians' throats and hurt their chests, and the earth felt like iron under their moccasins. Then the snow came, drifting over the hunting trails, and at last—the Ice King himself!

Nokome, in his wigwam, saw the giant at his door. The Ice King's hair was like a snowdrift. Icicles hung from his beard, and in his cold blue hand he held a glittering spear.

Bending his head with an icy clatter, he entered the wigwam, and when he spoke, his cold breath made Nokome shake from head to foot.

"Kwah-ee, Nokome!" The familiar Indian greeting sounded like ice shattering as it fell.

"Come up to the highest place," stuttered Nokome through chattering teeth, for it is a matter of pride with the Indian to treat any stranger in his home, friend or enemy, with politeness.

The Ice King took the honored place by the fire and seated himself with calm dignity, knowing he had only to

remain there a short time and Nokome would be dead of cold and exposure. Indeed, the youth's body already felt so stiff and chilled, he wondered if he could ever move again. Yet he must! Somehow he managed to stir his dull limbs and creep to the fire. He laid a few bits of wood on the dying flame and blew upon it feebly.

The Ice King smiled scornfully at his weak labors.

With enormous effort, Nokome managed to lift heavier boughs on the blaze, and now the flames began to crackle. Warmed a little, and moving more quickly now, Nokome added heavier and heavier logs, and the fire shot up higher.

The Ice King scowled and moved back a little.

Now Nokome, feeling life surge through him once more, heaped more and more wood upon the fire. The flames roared higher still, and the lodge grew hotter and hotter. The Ice King began to gasp, and great drops of sweat ran from his brow. Then at last Nokome took his precious store of sunflower oil and dashed it upon the fire. Up the flames shot with a roar, to the very peak of the wigwam!

The Ice King could bear it no longer. With a cry of rage and agony, he shrank back against the wall of the wigwam. Water streamed from his crown and his spear was melting quickly.

"Mercy!" gasped the giant. "Enough! You have won the victory. Now let me go!"

Nokome rose and raked away the fire.

"Go then," he cried triumphantly, "and know that, when

you return hereafter, we will always be ready for you."

"You have conquered me fairly," groaned the giant. "Twice! Now you are my master forever." And he fled from Nokome's lodge and away from the village.

Then amongst the Wabanaki there was great rejoicing. The people praised their Great Chief Glooscap for his wisdom, and made Nokome their village chief for his wit and courage. Never again would the Wabanaki fear the Ice King's power, for they had learned to turn Winter into Summer with their own hands.

And so, kespeadooksit—the story ends.

The Changing of Mikcheech

In an Indian village in the Old Time, there once lived a Micmac Indian named Mikcheech who was an old bachelor, very shabby and poor and, truth to tell, somewhat lazy. He lived all alone, having no wife to care for him, and his neighbors paid him no attention, for he was neither rich nor clever nor wise. Yet he bore his wants with great good humor, and Glooscap loved him for his cheerful, easy ways.

One day Glooscap came to the lodge of Mikcheech in the form of an ordinary Indian. Mikcheech hailed him with delight, for he was lonely and any stranger who came to his wigwam was sure of a welcome. He gave Glooscap the guest's place at the fire, shared with him his supper of fresh salmon and, after the meal, the two sat on either side of the fire, smoking and laughing and telling stories. Finally they sat together in contented silence until, suddenly, Glooscap asked his host why he had never married.

"Too lazy," Mikcheech admitted with a grin. "And now what maid would look at me, a homely old fellow with all his clothes full of holes!"

"You need a wife to mend those clothes," said Glooscap, "but first, I must turn tailor." And handing his magic belt to Mikcheech, he bade him put it on. No sooner was the belt clasped about the old fellow's waist than Mikcheech felt a change come over him. He looked down at himself in amazement. He was no longer a shabby old man, but a young and handsome brave in fine clothing.

"By the tail of the Beaver!" cried Mikcheech. "You can make a man over as easy as a suit of clothes!" But Glooscap shook his head.

"Not so. The outside of a man is easy, but the inside is another matter. It is hard to make over the whole of a man. Otherwise, I would not be so long at work in the world." Then Mikcheech knew his guest was Glooscap and was greatly alarmed.

"Fear not, Mikcheech," said the Great Chief, with a twinkle in his eye. "I am your friend. See now, I have done my part. The rest is up to you."

Then Mikcheech saw that Glooscap had played a fine trick on him. He had taken away his excuse for sitting about all day doing nothing. Now the lazy Mikcheech must stir himself to find a bride.

"Very well, Master," he said with his usual good humor. "I see my easy days are over. I shall get me a wife to keep me from idleness. But tell me, how long will my new form last?"

"As long as you are a man," said Glooscap. "Now, listen. There is a feast being held in the next village. Go there and choose a bride. I will await you here."

So Mikcheech went to the feast and the Indians made the handsome stranger welcome, inviting him to dance. They danced in the Micmac fashion, moving around in a circle, stamping their feet and uttering sharp cries, while a man in the center set the time on a *cheegumakun,* which is a drum of bark beaten with a stick.

Beyond the ring of male dancers sat the women watching. Mikcheech looked at them as he danced and saw the girl he wanted, the fairest of all in the village—Mahia, the Chief's youngest daughter. He knew immediately that no one else would do. He danced closer and ever closer to Mahia each time around the circle, until at the seventh round he was near enough to toss a small chip into her lap. Now this, in Micmac custom, was how a man declared his love. If the maid disdained him, she would frown and toss the chip away over her shoulder. If she returned his interest, she would smile and throw the chip back to him.

The dancers circled again, and once more Mikcheech drew near the Chief's daughter. To his joy, she smiled and flung the chip into his hands.

Mikcheech went straight to the Chief of the tribe and, looking meaningfully at Mahia, said, "I am tired of living alone." This is how the Micmacs ask for a girl's hand in marriage.

"You are a brave man," said the Chief, giving him a strange look, "but if it is your wish, you may have her. Come to the highest place, my son-in-law." And in this way Mikcheech and Mahia were married.

While his bride and her family prepared the wedding feast, Mikcheech hurried back to his own village to tell Glooscap of his good fortune, but Glooscap did not look happy.

"You have chosen unwisely, my friend," he said.

"Mahia is the loveliest maid in the village!" cried Mikcheech.

"For that reason," said Glooscap, "all the young men desire her. None have dared so far to ask her hand in marriage, for it is known that whoever wins her will be killed by the rest."

"Alas," sighed Mikcheech, "I am not much of a fighter. And I never like to exert myself unless it is absolutely necessary. However, I must have Mahia. Tell me what I must do."

"It is hard, as I told you, to change the whole of a man, but I can do even that. Are you willing to be changed?"

"Certainly," cried Mikcheech, "so long as I may have Mahia all my days."

"Very well," said Glooscap. "Do as I tell you, and before this day is through, you will be changed—and because you are patient and tough, you will be changed into a creature very hard to kill. Now listen closely."

Then Glooscap told Mikcheech that after the wedding feast there would be games. During the games, the young men would seek to slay him by crowding and trampling him to death.

"When they do this," said Glooscap, "it will be near your father-in-law's lodge, and to escape them you must jump over it."

Mikcheech was about to protest that he could never jump so high, but remembered in time that with Glooscap all things were possible.

"You will jump once, twice, three times," said the Great Chief, "and the third time will be terrible for you. But it must be. If you are patient and brave, no matter what happens, then you will become chief over a new race, and bear up a great nation."

Now all happened as Glooscap had foretold. The wedding of Mikcheech and Mahia was celebrated with a fine feast and dancing, and afterwards the young men played games. In the last game, the young men crowded against Mikcheech and tried to trip him. Then Mikcheech leapt like a bird over the Chief's lodge and all the braves gasped with astonishment. Soon recovering from their surprise, however, they drew their knives and hurried to the far side

of the lodge, but once more Mikcheech soared over the peak of the lodge.

"You'll have to jump high to catch me!" he cried merrily, and jumped for the third time.

This time, alas, Mikcheech caught on the crossed poles at the top of the lodge and hung there, helpless, dangling over the smoke-hole. The black smoke rolled up and enveloped him, staining his flesh and stinging his eyes.

"Oh, Master," groaned Mikcheech, "you are killing me!"

"Not so," he heard Glooscap say. "I am giving you new life. From this time, you will have no fear of knives. You will be able to roll through fire and never feel it. You will live in water as well as upon land."

Now the people could not see what was happening because of the smoke, nor could they understand the words of Glooscap, for he was invisible and spoke in a strange tongue which only Mikcheech could understand. Then the smoke rolled away and they saw Mikcheech again, but terribly changed. His head was green, his hands and feet all wrinkled, and his back was a hard shell streaked with smoke stains. He had become a turtle!

No one had ever seen such a creature before, but they knew it must be Mikcheech and they were just as determined as ever to kill him. So, thrusting poles up from inside the lodge, they knocked him down.

Now, although Mikcheech was no longer a man, and no longer handsome, he was as good-humored as ever. He held no grudge against Glooscap for turning him into an animal and thought it a very good joke. Remembering what the Great Chief had foretold, he decided to turn the joke on the Indians who were trying to kill him. So he pretended to be terribly frightened, begging the young men with tears in his eyes not to kill him.

They, seeing his shell was much too hard to pierce with a knife, made to cut off his head—but Mikcheech pulled his head into his shell out of harm's way. Then the braves decided to kill him by fire.

"No, no—please don't burn me," begged Mikcheech with

pretended terror. "Anything but that!"

But the heartless youths built a huge fire and flung him into the midst of the flames. To their amazement, the turtle turned over lazily and went to sleep, and when the fire had burned down a little, he woke and called for more wood, saying he was cold! Angrily, the young men dragged him from the fire and declared they would drown him instead. Hearing this, Mikcheech began to struggle mightily.

"Oh, oh! Please don't do that. Shoot me with arrows, burn me with fire, but don't drown me! You don't know how I dread water!"

The braves laughed and dragged him to the water's edge. Mikcheech fought lustily, tearing up trees and roots and screaming like a madman, but they bore him into a canoe and paddled out beyond the breakers where the water was deep. Then they flung him into the water and watched him sink.

"Now we are rid of him," they said, and returned to shore to tell Mahia her husband was dead. Poor Mahia ran to the water's edge and wept for her lost bridegroom.

On the following day, the braves saw something on a rock far out at sea. Deciding it might be something good to eat, they went a-fishing, but as they came near the rock, they saw it was Mikcheech stretched out lazily in the sun!

"As you see, my friends," he laughed at them, "I am enjoying my new home," and, rolling over into the water, he dived down into the green depths, as all turtles do when danger approaches. Then the young men knew they were defeated and had no power over him.

However, though Mikcheech was now safe from his foes, he was even lonelier than he had been before Glooscap changed him. The fish and the gulls were his only companions, and he longed for speech with his own kind.

"Oh, Glooscap," he sighed in his loneliness, "you promised I should have Mahia for my wife and become chief over a new nation."

There was no reply, but as he rose to the top of the waves and looked around, Mikcheech saw a gray-green shape swimming towards him and heard a familiar voice.

"It is I," the voice said, "Mahia, your wife." The voice came from another turtle. Glooscap had changed Mahia too.

Now in the course of time Mahia gave Mikcheech many fine children. And so, as Glooscap had promised, Mikcheech became father and chief over a new race—the race of turtles—and never was lonely again.

And there, kespeadooksit—the story ends.

How the Rabbit Lost His Tail

You have heard how Glooscap came to rule over the Wabanaki and how he made the animals, and how at first some of them were treacherous and disobedient. In time, however, he gave posts of honor to those whom he could trust, and they were proud to be Glooscap's servants. Two dogs became his watchmen, and the loon his messenger and talebearer. And, because the rabbit had the kindest heart of all the animals in the forest, Glooscap made Ableegumooch his forest guide.

Now in those days Ableegumooch the Rabbit was a very different animal than he is today. His body was large and round, his legs were straight and even, and he had a long bushy tail. He could run and walk like other animals, not with a hop-hop-hop as he does today.

One day in springtime, when the woods were carpeted with star flowers and lillies-of-the-valley, and the ferns were waist-high, Ableegumooch lay resting beside a fallen log. Hearing a rustle on the path, he peered around his log to see who was coming. It was Uskool the Fisher, a large animal of the weasel tribe, and he was weeping.

"What is the matter with him," wondered the rabbit, who was inquisitive as well as soft-hearted. He popped his head up over the log and Uskool nearly jumped out of his fur with surprise. "It's only me—Ableegumooch," said the rabbit. "Do you mind telling me why you are crying?"

"Oh, greetings, Ableegumooch," sighed Uskool, when he had recovered from his fright. "I'm going to my wedding."

"And that makes you cry?" asked the astonished rabbit.

"Of course not," said Uskool. "I've lost my way, that's the trouble."

"Well, just take your time," said the rabbit sensibly, "and you'll soon find it again."

"But I have no time to spare," groaned the fisher. "My future father-in-law has sworn that if I do not arrive for the wedding by sunset today, he will marry his daughter to Kakakooch the Crow. And, look, already the sun is low in the sky!"

"In that case," said Ableegumooch, "I'd better show you the way. Where are you going?"

"To a village called Wilnech," said Uskool eagerly, "near the bend in the river!"

"I know it well," said the rabbit. "Just follow me."

"Thanks, Ableegumooch," cried the happy fisher. "Now I shall be sure to arrive in time."

So off they went on their journey. Uskool, who was not very quick on the ground, being more accustomed to travel in the trees, moved slowly.

"You go ahead," he told the impatient rabbit, "and I'll follow as fast as I can."

So Ableegumooch ran ahead, and sometimes all Uskool could see of him was his long bushy tail whisking through the trees. So it was that Uskool, looking far ahead and not watching where he stepped, fell suddenly headfirst into a deep pit.

His cries soon brought Ableegumooch running back, and seeing the fisher's trouble, he cried out cheerfully, "Never mind. I'll get you out."

He let his long tail hang down inside the pit.

"Catch hold, and hang on tight, while I pull."

Uskool held on to the rabbit's tail, and Ableegumooch strained mightily to haul him up. Alas, the weight of the fisher was too great. With a loud snap, the rabbit's tail broke off short, within an inch of the root, and there was poor Ableegumooch with hardly any tail at all!

Now you would think that this might have discouraged the rabbit from helping Uskool, but not so. When Ableegumooch made up his mind to do something for somebody, he did it. Holding on to a stout tree with his front paws, he lowered his hinder part into the pit.

"Take hold of my legs," he cried, "and hang on tight. I'll soon pull you out."

Ableegumooch pulled and he pulled until his waist was drawn out thin, and he could feel his hind legs stretching and stretching—and soon he feared he might lose them too. But at last, just as he thought he must give up, the fisher's head rose above the edge of the pit and he scrambled to safety.

"Well!" said the rabbit as he sat down to catch his breath. "My waist isn't so round as it was, and my hind legs seem a good bit longer than they were. I believe it will make walking rather difficult."

And sure enough, it did. When the rabbit tried to walk, he tumbled head over heels. Finally, to get along at all, he had to hop.

"Oh, well," said the rabbit, "hopping is better than nothing," and after a little practice, he found he could hop quite fast. And so they hurried on through the forest.

At last, just before the sun touched the rim of the trees, they arrived at the bride's village. All the fishers were gathered, waiting, and they smiled and cheered at sight of Uskool and his guide—all but Kakakooch the Crow, who was far from glad to see them! In fact, as soon as he saw Uskool take the bride's hand, he flew out of the village in a temper, and never came back again. But nobody cared about him.

Ableegumooch was the most welcome guest at the wedding when Uskool told the other fishers what he had done. All was feasting and merriment, and the rabbit danced with the bride so hard she fell into a bramble bush and tore her gown. She was in a dreadful state when she found she was not fit to be seen in company, and ran to hide behind a tree. The rabbit was terribly sorry and wanted to help her, so he hopped away to get a caribou skin he had seen drying in the sun, and made a new dress out of it for the bride.

"You must have a fine girdle to go with it," said he, and he cut a thin strip off the end of the skin. Then he put one end of the strip in his mouth and held the other end with his front paws, twisting the strip into a fancy cord. He twisted and twisted, and he twisted it so hard the cord snapped out of his teeth and split his upper lip right up to his nose! And now you see why it is that rabbits are harelipped!

"Never mind," said Ableegumooch, when the bride wept at his mishap, "it can't be helped," and he gave her the cord just as it was, to tie around her waist.

"Wait right here," said the bride, and she ran off. In a moment she was back, carrying a lovely white fur coat.

"This is for you," she said shyly. "It is the color of the snow, so if you wear it in winter, your enemies will not be able to see you."

Ableegumooch was delighted with his present and promised not to put it on till the snow came, as his brown coat would hide him better in summer. The wedding was over now, and he said good-bye to Uskool and the bride, and started for home.

Now it happened that before he had gone far, he came to a small pool in the woods, so smooth it was like a mirror. Looking into it, the rabbit saw himself for the first time since his accidents, and was aghast. Was this he—this creature with the split lip, the hind legs stretched out of shape, and a tail like a blob of down?

"Oh dear, oh dear," sobbed Ableegumooch, "how can I face my friends looking like this?" Then, in his misery, he remembered Glooscap, his Master. "O Master! See what has happened to your poor guide. I'm not fit to be seen any more, except to laugh at. Please put me back to my former shape."

High up on Blomidon, Glooscap heard the rabbit and came striding down from his lodge to see what was wrong. When he saw poor Ableegumooch, all out of shape, he had all he could do to keep from laughing, though of course he kept a sober face so as not to hurt the rabbit's feelings.

"Come now," he said, "things may not be as bad as you think. You know how fond you are of clover, Ableegumooch?"

The rabbit nodded piteously.

"And you know how hard it is to find. Well, with that long cleft in your lip, you will be able to smell clover even when it is miles away!"

"That's good," said the rabbit, cheering up a little, "but it's very uncomfortable having to hop everywhere I go."

"Perhaps, for a time," said Glooscap, "but have you noticed how much faster you hop than you used to run?"

The rabbit did a little hop, and a jump or two, just to see.

"Why I believe you're right!" he cried, but then his face fell again. "But my tail, Master! I mind that most of all. I was so proud of it."

"It was certainly a handsome tail," admitted the Great

Chief, "but recall how it used to catch in thorns and brambles."

"That's true!" cried the rabbit, excitedly, "and it was very awkward when Wokwes the Fox was chasing me! Now I can slip through the narrowest places with no trouble at all!" And he laughed with delight. "Why—with my new legs, my cleft lip, and without my long tiresome tail, I'm a better rabbit than I was before!"

"So you are!" said Glooscap, and at last he was able to laugh. When Glooscap laughs heartily, the land shakes and the trees bend over, so the rabbit had to hold on tightly to a tree to keep from being knocked over. "So you are indeed!" laughed Glooscap.

And that is why the rabbit and the rabbit's children, and his children's children have had, ever since that day, a little white scut of a tail, a cleft lip, and long hind legs on which they can hop all day and never tire. And since then, too, in winter, rabbits wear white coats.

And thus, kespeadooksit—the story ends.

Oochigeas and the Invisible Boy

THERE WAS once a Malicete Indian village on the edge of a lake in the land of the Wabanaki, and in this village lived three sisters. The two older girls, Oona and Abit, were handsome and proud, but the youngest, whom they called Oochigeas, was timid and plain. She suffered much from the selfishness of her sisters, but bore all their ill-treatment without complaint.

Because these girls had no parents, they were given meat by the tribe's hunters in return for making pottery. Through much practice, they had become the best makers of pots in the village. And this is how they made them. First Oona, the eldest, wove a basket from ash splints, then Abit lined it with wet clay. Finally, it was given to the youngest girl to harden in the fire. As the clay slowly baked, the wind blew the fire into Oochigeas' face, and in time her hair was singed close to her head and her face covered with burns. And that is why her sisters mocked her with the name of Oochigeas, which means "little scarred one."

Now Glooscap the Great Chief knew all his People. He saw the misery of Oochigeas and pitied her, and he scowled at the cruelty of her sisters—yet he did nothing. And this was something that Marten, his servant, could not understand.

"My elder brother," said Marten, "though she is plain, her heart is kind. Can you not help her?"

"We will see," said the Great Chief with a wise nod. "Oochigeas must help herself first. Kindness is a great virtue, but courage is the first rule of my People."

Now on the far side of the lake, remote from the village, there lived an Indian youth called Team, who had the wonderful power of making himself invisible. To all save his sister he was as the rustle of a leaf in the forest, a sigh of wind in the treetops, or a breath of air in the heavens. His name meant "moose" and the moose was his *teomul*, or charm, that gave him his power. Having this magical power, Team needed no bow and arrow. He could walk straight up to game, without being seen or heard, and slay it with his bare hands.

One day, Team's sister appeared in the village.

"My brother is tired of living alone," she said to the people. "Team will marry the first girl who is able to see him."

Now, though no person had seen Team, or knew if he was tall or short, fat or thin, plain or handsome, yet they knew of his magic power and his great success in hunting. To the Indians, who live by hunting, a brave who can keep meat in his lodge all the time is admired above all others. He is a kind of prince. It is no wonder that every maiden in the village yearned to become the bride of the Invisible Boy.

All the unmarried maidens were eager to try their fortune and, one after another, each made a visit to the lodge across the lake. And, one after another, each came back disappointed. At last, all had made the attempt except the three sisters.

"Now it is my turn," said Oona. "I'm sure *I* shall be able to see him."

"You indeed!" sniffed Abit. "I'm as likely to see him as you are. Why should you go first?"

"I am the eldest!"

"Team is sure to want a younger woman!"

The two sisters glared at each other.

"You needn't think I shall let you go alone," declared Oona angrily.

"Then we'll go together," said Abit. And so they did.

Dressing themselves in their finest robes, they set off for the lodge across the lake. Team's sister received them kindly and took them to the wigwam to rest after their journey. Then, when it was time for her brother's return, she led them to the shore.

"Do you see my brother?" she asked.

The two girls gazed eagerly out over the lake. They saw a canoe approaching, but though it moved swiftly through the water, it appeared to be empty! No paddle could be seen, for whatever Team held or wore became also invisible.

Abit thought to herself that she would pretend to see him, and Team's sister would never know the difference.

"I see him!" she cried.

And Oona, not to be outdone, echoed, "Yes! I see him too!"

Team's sister knew that at least one of the girls lied, for only one maiden would be allowed to see her brother and that would be his future bride.

"Of what is his shoulder strap made?" she asked.

The two girls thought for a moment. They knew that, generally, Indians used rawhide or withe for their shoulder straps.

"A strip of rawhide," guessed Abit.

"No—withe!" cried Oona.

Then Team's sister knew that neither had seen her brother and she resolved to punish them for their dishonesty.

"Very well," she said quietly. "Come to the wigwam and help me prepare my brother's supper."

The two girls were anxious to know which of them had given the correct answer, so they followed Team's sister and helped her prepare the meal. Each hoped that she alone would see Team when he came. When all was ready, the sister of Team warned the girls not to sit in her brother's place but to remain on her side of the fire. Then, looking up, she greeted her brother—but the girls could see no one.

"Take my brother's load of meat," she told Abit, who looked around her in dismay. As long as the meat was on Team's shoulder, it could not be seen. Suddenly, a great load of venison dropped from nowhere on Abit's toes. Abit screamed and ran from the lodge in pain and fright. Now Team's sister told Oona to remove her brother's wet moccasins and put them to dry. Of course Oona could not do so. A pair of wet moccasins came suddenly sailing through the air and slapped her across the face. Then Oona too ran away, crying with mortification.

"My bride is a long time coming," sighed Team. "And those were very fine looking girls."

"Patience, my brother. You must have one who is brave and truthful, as well as lovely, and such a one has not come yet."

Abit and Oona returned home to vent their rage and spite on poor Oochigeas. To escape their cruelty, she fled to the woods and there, in a secluded spot, relieved her heart with tears. But when there were no tears left, and her spirit had been calmed by the peace of the forest, Oochigeas began to think. Now that her sisters had failed, she was the only maid left in the village who had not tried to see the Invisible Boy. Yet, if her fine sisters had failed, what chance had she, poor and plain as she was? A great hunter like Team would not wish a scar-faced girl like Oochigeas for a bride. All the same, hope stirred in her breast. Her heart began to beat fast at the thought of going to Team's lodge. She had no fine clothes to wear. Her sisters might try to stop her. The people would laugh. It would take courage—

Her mind was made up!

Oochigeas gathered sheets of birchbark and cut out a gown and cap and leggings, and sewed them together with grass. The clothing was stiff and awkward, and it crackled when she walked, but it covered her. Then she went home and found a pair of Oona's discarded moccasins. They were huge on her small feet and she had to tie them on by winding the strings around her ankles. She was truly an odd-looking sight, and her two sisters stared at her in amazement.

"Where are you going in that ridiculous outfit?" Oona asked.

"I am going to Team's lodge," answered Oochigeas.

"What! You foolish girl! Come back!"

"Oh, let her go," said Abit. "Let the people see her and she'll come back soon enough, in tears."

Oochigeas' way lay through the village, and the men and boys shouted and jeered at her.

"Shame, shame!"

"Ugly creature!"

"See how her burned hair sticks out from her cap!"

"Why does she wear birchbark instead of skins?"

"Come back, Oochigeas. Where do you think you're

going? To see Team?" And they laughed so hard they rolled on the ground.

But, though her heart burned with shame, Oochigeas pretended not to hear, and walked on with her head high, until she was out of their sight. Then she hurried through the woods and around the edge of the lake, trying not to think of the ordeal ahead. Doubtless Team's sister would laugh at her too. Still she went on, and came at last to the lodge and saw Team's sister at the door.

"I have come," gasped Oochigeas before the other could speak, "I have come—to see Team—if I can." And she looked pleadingly at Team's sister.

"Come in and rest," said the sister of Team gently, and Oochigeas nearly wept at the unexpected kindness, but she managed to retain her dignity as they waited in silence for the sun to go down. Then Team's sister led her to the lake.

"Do you see my brother?" she asked.

Oochigeas looked and saw a canoe, empty. She heard the dip of a paddle and the swish of the water at the bow, but though she gazed with all her might, she saw no one. She whispered with a sinking heart, "No, I cannot see him."

"Look again," urged Team's sister, out of pity, and because the girl had so far been truthful. Oochigeas gazed once more at the canoe, and suddenly gave a gasp.

"Oh! Yes! Now I see him!"

"If you see him," said Team's sister quickly, "of what is his shoulder strap made?"

"Why it is made of a rainbow," marveled Oochigeas, and Team's sister knew her brother had found his bride. She led the girl back to the wigwam and stripped off her ugly

clothes, bathed her, and dressed her in doeskin, then gave her a comb to tidy her hair.

"Alas," thought Oochigeas, "I have so little hair to comb," but as she drew the comb against her head, she found to her amazement that her hair had grown suddenly long and thick. Moreover, the scars had gone from her face. She was beautiful!

Then the handsome Team came, laughing, and crying out, "At last I've found you, my lovely bride." And he led

her to the wife's place in the wigwam. And from that day on, Oochigeas and Team, and Team's sister, lived out their days in peace and happiness.

Far away on Blomidon, Glooscap looked at Marten with a wise smile. He had known all along, you see, that Oochigeas had courage under her gentleness—and a brave spirit makes all things possible.

And so it happened. Kespeadooksit.

Ableegumooch, the Lazy Rabbit

In the Old Time, as you know, Ableegumooch was Glooscap's forest guide and helped wayfarers lost in the forest. However, as time went on, Indians and animals learned to find their own way through the trees and did not need the rabbit's services so often. Ableegumooch grew fat and lazy. If there was something easy and pleasant to do, he did it. If the thing were difficult or tiring, he did not. Now that is no way to keep a wigwam stocked with food. Often, poor old Noogumee, his grandmother, with whom he lived, had to hunt for food herself, or they would have gone hungry. And no matter how much she scolded him, Ableegumooch refused to mend his ways.

Glooscap, far away in his lodge on Blomidon, saw that the rabbit was becoming a thoroughly useless creature. He must be warned against the dangers of laziness. So, wasting no time, Glooscap descended from his lodge to the beach in three huge strides, launched his canoe, and paddled across the Bay of Fundy to the shore near the rabbit's home.

It was a fine bright morning, the air cool and tasting of salt, as it always does in the Maritime Provinces. And presently along hopped the rabbit, singing with fine spirit:

It's a lovely day to do
Nothing, nothing
All the day through!

He paid no attention to the tasty leaves and berries he might have been gathering for dinner. He was much more interested in watching other people work. There was Miko the Squirrel scampering up the big maple tree, his cheeks bulged out with nuts, pausing only long enough to scold Ableegumooch for coming too near his storehouse. There was Mechipchamooech the Bumble Bee, busy at the goldenrod, gathering honey for his hive. And there was Teetees the Blue Jay, flying worms to his family in the big pine. It was all so interesting that Ableegumooch stopped beside a stately fir tree to enjoy the scene. Suddenly behind him, he heard a voice.

"Ableegumooch, be careful!"

The rabbit jumped and whirled about, but there was nobody there. The voice spoke again, from somewhere over his head.

"Take care, Ableegumooch, or your lazy ways will bring you pain and sorrow."

The rabbit looked up and saw the fir tree shake like a leaf in a storm, yet not a breath of wind stirred. Frightened out of his wits, he ran—and he never stopped running until he was safe at home, where he told his grandmother what had happened.

"Glooscap has given you a warning," said his grandmother. "Be sure to obey him, grandson, or you will be sorry."

The rabbit's legs were still trembling from fright and exertion, and he promised at once that he would take care to mend his lazy ways in future. And indeed, for a while, he went busily about his hunting and kept the wigwam well stocked with food. But, when autumn came, he grew lazy again and went back to his old careless ways.

It's a lovely day to do
Nothing, nothing
All the day through!

So sang Ableegumooch as he sauntered through the glory of autumn trees. Noogumee begged and scolded and pleaded, but he continued to spend more time visiting his neighbors than gathering food. One day, when winter had come to the land, he came to the wigwam of Keoonik the Otter. Keoonik politely asked him to dine, and the rabbit promptly accepted. Keoonik turned to his elderly housekeeper and addressed her in the usual Indian fashion:

"Noogumee, prepare the meal."

Then he took some fishhooks and went off, the rabbit hopping along behind, curious to see what he was going to do. Keeonik sat on the snowy bank of the river and slid down an icy path into the water. In a moment, he reappeared with a string of eels which he carried to his grandmother, and she promptly cooked them for dinner.

"Gracious!" thought Ableegumooch. "If that isn't an easy way to get a living. I can do that as well as Keoonik," and he invited the otter to be his guest at dinner on the following day. Then he hurried home.

"Come," he said to his grandmother, "we are going to move our lodge down to the river." And in spite of all she could say, he insisted on moving it. Noogumee reminded him that the wigwam was empty of food, and he ought to be out hunting, but Ableegumooch paid no attention. He was busy making a slide like Keoonik's. The weather was cold, so all he had to do was pour water down the snowy bank, where it soon froze, and there was his fishing slide. Early next day, the guest arrived. When it was time for dinner, Ableegumooch said to his grandmother:

"Noogumee, prepare the meal."

"There is nothing to prepare," said she, sadly.

"Oh, I will see to that," said the rabbit with a confident laugh, and he took his place at the top of the slide to go fishing. When he tried to push off, however, he found it was not so easy. His coat was rough and bulky and dry, not smooth and slippery like the otter's. He had to wriggle and push with his heels until at last he slid down and plunged into the water. The cold took his breath quite away, and he suddenly remembered he was unable to swim. Struggling and squealing, he thought no more of fishing, for he was in great danger of drowning.

"What on earth is the matter with him?" Keoonik asked the grandmother.

"I suppose he has seen someone else do that," sighed Noogumee, "and he thinks he can do it too."

Keoonik helped the freezing, half-drowned rabbit out of the water and, since there was nothing to eat, went home hungry and disgusted.

But do you think that cold bath cured Ableegumooch? Not at all. The very next day, as he ran idly through the forest, he came to the lodge of some female woodpeckers. He was delighted when these Antawaas invited him to dinner.

He watched eagerly to see how they found food.

One of the woodpeckers took a dish, went up the side of an old beech tree and quickly dug out a plentiful supply of food, which was cooked and placed before the rabbit.

"My, oh my!" thought Ableegumooch. "How easily some people get a living. What is to prevent me from getting mine in that fashion?" And he told the Antawaas they must come and dine with him.

On the day following, they appeared at the rabbit's lodge and Ableegumooch said to his grandmother importantly:

"Noogumee, prepare the meal."

"You foolish rabbit," said she, "there is nothing to prepare."

"Make the fire," said the rabbit grandly, "and I shall see to the rest."

He took the stone point from an eel spear and fastened it on his head in imitation of a woodpecker's bill, then climbed a tree and began knocking his head against it. Soon his head was bruised and bleeding, and he lost his hold and fell to the earth with a tremendous crash. The Antawaas could not keep from laughing.

"Pray what was he doing up there?"

"I suppose he has seen someone else do that," said Noogumee, shaking her head, "and thinks he can do it too." And she advised them to go home, as there would be no food for them there that day.

Now, sore as he was, you would certainly think the rabbit had learned his lesson. Yet, a day or two later, he was idling in the woods as usual when he came upon Mooin the Bear, who invited him to dinner. He was greatly impressed at the way in which the bear got his meal. Mooin merely took a sharp knife and cut small pieces off the soles of his feet. These he placed in a kettle on the fire, and in a short while they enjoyed a delicious meal.

"This must be the easiest way of all to get a dinner,"

marveled Ableegumooch, and he invited Mooin to dine with him next day. Now what the rabbit did not know was that the bears preserve food on their feet. They press ripe blueberries with their paws and, after the cakes have dried upon them, cut bits off to eat. The silly rabbit thought Mooin had actually cut pieces off his paws!

At the appointed time, Ableegumooch ordered his grandmother to prepare the meal, and when she said there was nothing to prepare, he told her to put the kettle on and he would do the rest. Then he took a stone knife and began to cut at his feet as he had seen Mooin do. But oh dear me, it hurt. It hurt dreadfully! With tears streaming down his cheeks, he hacked and hacked, first at one foot and then at the other. Mooin the Bear was greatly astonished.

"What on earth is the fellow trying to do?" he asked.

Noogumee shook her head dismally.

"It is the same old thing. He has seen someone else do this."

"Well!" said Mooin crossly, "It is most insulting to be asked to dinner and get nothing to eat. The trouble with that fellow is—he's lazy!" and he went home in a huff.

Then at last, Ableegumooch, nursing his sore feet, remembered what Glooscap had said. All at once, he saw how silly he had been.

"Oh dear!" he said. "My own ways of getting food are hard, but others' are harder. I shall stick to my own in the future," and he did.

From then on, the wigwam of Ableegumooch and his grandmother was always well stored with food, winter and summer, and though he still sings, his song has changed:

> It's a wiser thing to be
> Busy, busy
> Constantly!

And far away on Blomidon, Glooscap, seeing his foolish rabbit mend his ways at last, set a light to his pipe and smoked contentedly.

And, kespeadooksit—the story ends.

Badger and the Green Giant

THERE WAS in the Old Time a great rogue named Badger. The Wabanaki storytellers, who talk of men as though they were animals and animals as though they were men, sometimes spoke of Badger as a man and sometimes as an animal. It was agreed, however, that he had something of Lox in him—Lox, you remember, who was the son of Evil and who sometimes took on the form of a badger. And that is how this Indian known as Badger got his name.

Now this fearless and impudent rascal lived a carefree life on the labor of others, having no time from merrymaking to spend on hunting. In time, however, his neighbors grew tired of supporting him. One summer when food was scarce, the Chief of Badger's tribe said to him:

"You take all and give nothing. We can no longer afford

to share our meat with you. This is what we have decided. You will be given food for half a moon's journey. You will then be too far away to trouble us, and must live as you can."

For once, Badger's face lost its grin.

"Who will take care of Little Brother when I'm gone?" he demanded. Now you see, Badger was not all bad. He had a small brother who was gentle and shy and not very clever, and ever since the boys had lost their parents, Badger had looked after Little Brother and treated him with affection.

"He will be given a home with foster parents," said the Chief, but Little Brother burst into tears.

"I want to go with my elder brother," he wailed.

"Very well, come along," said Badger, and grinned saucily at the people. "Thanks, my friends, for giving us a chance to see the world!" Then, with all their possessions in a blanket slung over Badger's shoulder, the two set jauntily off into the woods. However, they did not go far. Badger stopped before the mouth of a small cave and told Little Brother to go inside.

"This food will last you until the full of the moon, when I shall return," he said. "I must play one last trick on our late friends!"

Then Badger dressed himself in the beads and feathers of a medicine man and put a mask on his face. Medicine men, you know, were the doctors of the Indians. Some of them understood how to make medicine from herbs and how to cure people; but others, like Badger, were frauds.

He knew that his former tribe had no medicine man at present, so he went back to the village and announced that he was a powerful man of magic. Not recognizing Badger behind the mask, his old neighbors treated him with great respect. They gave him a wigwam to live in and shared their food with him, begging him to treat their sick and use his magic to make meat more plentiful.

For a while, Badger played the medicine man with glee. He beat his drum and shook his rattle, and pretended to summon spirits. He sold charms and fell into trances, and all the time behind his mask, he was laughing. However, game in the district grew scarcer and scarcer, and as the people grew hungrier, they began to lose faith in the medicine man. If he was really a magician, why did he not make hunting better?

One day, near the full of the moon, a long loud wail came from the forest. The Indians shook with fear, but not Badger, who knew at once what it meant. It was Little Brother crying because he was lonely and his food was gone. The wail came again.

"It is the giant, Famine," said Badger with a long face. "He says he is coming to this village."

Then all the people began to groan with dismay, for when Famine comes, he brings death by starvation.

"Never fear," said Badger calmly, "for I, your medicine man, will go out to meet him and drive him away."

The people exclaimed with gratitude and admiration.

"Give me a bag of tallow," said Badger, "to take with me, for I shall need plenty of strength to defeat that fellow."

Tallow was a kind of fat, a great delicacy with the Indians in olden times. It was made by pounding and breaking the bones of a moose, then boiling the bones until the grease came to the top. The grease, a white substance as hard as wax, was then skimmed off with a wooden spoon. It was so nourishing, hunters used to take it with them on long hunting expeditions as their only provision.

So the people gave Badger a large bag of tallow, the last they had, and off he went, crying out in a commanding voice, "Ahhh Chowwwaaa!" The Indians thought this a cry of defiance against the giant, but it was really the secret name Badger had for his brother, to let him know he was coming.

They waited and listened, but heard no sound of battle. They waited long—and in vain—for the return of their medicine man.

Meanwhile, deep in the forest, Badger and Little Brother were feasting on the tallow, laughing together at Badger's cleverness, when suddenly they heard a rushing sound in the forest. Badger jumped up, alarmed, as huge feet came crashing through the underbrush. The trees swayed as a great hand flung them aside, and all at once a fearsome giant stood before the brothers. His face was as green as the grass, and his hair sprang out from his huge head like needles on pine boughs. Before Badger knew what was happening, the Green Giant had seized Little Brother in his mighty green

hand and had stuffed him into the bag he carried on his shoulder.

"Save me," shrieked Little Brother.

Badger rushed upon the giant furiously, biting and punching and kicking, but the giant only laughed.

"What is tickling my legs?" he asked.

"Give me back my Little Brother," stormed Badger.

"Certainly," said the Green Giant, "as soon as you bring me the magic food of Glooscap which never grows less, no matter how much of it is eaten."

Poor Badger stared at the giant in dismay. It was a long way to Blomidon where Glooscap lived, and the path to it was full of danger. Moreover, there was no certainty of Glooscap giving him the food when he got there.

"I shall wait for you here," the Green Giant shouted, "but only for the space of time it takes the sun to run its full course. If you do not bring the food by then, I shall have to eat Little Brother instead."

Without a word, Badger turned and set off through the trees at top speed. Late that same day, tired and breathless, he reached the shore of Minas Basin and looked up at Blomidon's red slopes, immense against the darkening sky. He knew, in order to find Glooscap's lodge, he must climb to the very top. He was terribly tired, and yearned to rest, but the thought of Little Brother in the hands of the Green Giant drove him up the red slope as fast as possible.

The red stone was slippery and covered him with red dust, but he kept on. Branches of low spruce and juniper scratched his face and tore his hands, but he paid no attention. His lungs pained, his head throbbed. His throat was hot and dry as he dragged himself the last few yards, and tumbled over full length on the grass at the summit. Too worn out for a moment to move, Badger lay still, recovering his breath. Then he got wearily to his feet. There stood Glooscap's great wigwam, a fire glowing dimly within. The Great Chief himself was nowhere in sight, nor was there any sign of Noogumee, Glooscap's grandmother, or of Marten his servant. Badger could not wait for their return to ask for the food—there was no time. Besides, the Great Chief might refuse to give it to him. Badger must get the food somehow and hurry back to the Green Giant.

He crept into the lodge and looked around, then cried out softly with triumph. A dish of Glooscap's magic food stood beside the fire. He had only to reach out and take it; but as his fingers curved around the dish they were struck aside.

"Stop, thief!" a stern voice commanded. And Badger looked up to see the great Glooscap towering over him. But his fear for Little Brother was even greater than his fear of the Great Chief.

"Please, Master!" he cried. "Give me the magic food. I must save my brother from the Green Giant."

"Why should I give you anything," asked Glooscap, "you

who have robbed and made fun of your neighbors?"

"You can't let Little Brother die," Badger cried. "It wasn't his fault. If you don't help me, the giant will eat him!"

"Will he?" asked Glooscap mysteriously, and before Badger's surprised eyes, his shape began to change. His skin became green, his hair stood out from his head in green spikes, and his green face assumed a ferocious expression.

"The Green Giant was you all the time!" gasped Badger.

"And I hope he has taught you a lesson," said Glooscap, resuming his own appearance. "Are you sorry for the way you have behaved?"

"Yes, indeed," cried Badger.

"And will you promise to give up your silly tricks and do your share of the hunting?"

"I will, I will, if only—"

"Then look behind you."

Badger turned and saw Little Brother, smiling and unharmed, standing beside the fire. So great was Badger's relief, he nearly cried. For the first time, too, he realized how tired he was, and how hungry. The old impudent grin reappeared.

"I don't suppose," he suggested, "you could spare *me* a taste of that food?"

"Certainly *not!*" said Glooscap indignantly, "not until you can share it with the people you robbed of their tallow. Take this food to them at once. It will never grow less, no matter how much is eaten, until game is again plentiful in the forest."

When the people of Badger's old village saw him bringing the magic food of Glooscap, they forgave him and welcomed him back into the tribe. Famine no longer troubled the Indians, and Badger behaved himself for quite some time.

But if you think he had played his last trick, you are much mistaken, for you will hear again in time of Badger—and his mischief-making.

Until then, kespeadooksit!

Glooscap, the Trickster

IN THE Old Time of Glooscap's People, a poor Indian widow and her son Tabulech lived in a wigwam by themselves at some distance from a Malicete village. Tabulech was a good lad, but awkward with bow and arrow. He could not shoot straight if his life depended upon it. He and his mother, therefore, had to live as best they could by trapping and fishing. With hard work, they could just manage, but there was never anything left over.

Now the Chief of the nearby village demanded a yearly tribute of wampum from all who lived within reach of his hand. Wampum, you know, is a kind of Indian money made of shells, and the Indians used it in trading. The people feared the Malicete chief because he claimed to be a magician and threatened to put an evil spell on the people if they refused to pay.

At the time of our story, the tribute was nearly due, and Tabulech and his mother had not a single piece of wampum in their lodge. In desperation, the mother took a treasured moosehide left to her by her husband and told Tabulech to go to the village and trade it for wampum.

So off Tabulech went, with the moosehide over his shoulder. He had not gone far when he met an old man, who raised his hand and said politely, "Kwah-ee, my son."

Tabulech returned the greeting with equal politeness.

"I see you have a fine moosehide there," said the old man. "I am in need of just such an article. Will you give it to me?"

Tabulech was sorry to refuse, but explained to the old man that he must sell the hide to get wampum for the tribute.

"Listen now," the old man said coaxingly. "I'll trade you this dish of food for it."

Tabulech looked at the dish and saw a tiny portion of ground cooked meal, hardly enough for a good swallow, and shook his head. The old man shrugged and said cheerfully, "Oh, very well then, but taste a little before you go."

Out of politeness, Tabulech did so, and found to his surprise that it was delicious.

"Have some more," offered the old man slyly.

"Willingly!" cried Tabulech, and went on eating. To his amazement, no matter how much he ate (and he ate a great deal) there was just as much left in the dish. He ate and he ate, and at last he had eaten all he wanted and wished to stop. Then, to his horror, he found he had to keep on eating just the same.

Oh, how the old man laughed to see Tabulech try to push the dish away, at the same time grabbing the food and stuffing it into his mouth. He laughed till the tears came.

"Come," said the old man gaspingly. "Give me the moosehide and you may stop eating. Moreover, you may have the dish of food to keep."

By this time Tabulech felt he might burst if he ate another mouthful, so he gladly gave the moosehide to the old fellow, and taking the dish of food in exchange, walked sadly home to his mother to tell her what had happened.

Now I'll tell you something Tabulech did not know. The old man he had met was none other than Glooscap, disguised. The Great Chief was something of a trickster, you see, and loved now and then to play jokes on his People, especially when by so doing he could help them.

The next day, Tabulech was sent off with another prized article, a fine bearskin. His mother bid him get a better bargain than he had the day before. However, there on the path again was the old man, holding a shabby old belt in his hand.

"Will you trade this belt for that skin?"

Tabulech took a firmer grip on his fine bearskin.

"I should say not! I am not such a fool as that!"

Instantly the belt jumped out of the old man's hand and wrapped itself around Tabulech, squeezing him and squeezing him until he cried for mercy.

"Take it off, take it off!"

"The belt will come off quick enough," the old man chuckled, "when I have that bearskin in my hand." So, to keep from having the last breath squeezed out of him, Tabulech was obliged to trade the skin for the belt. His mother was scandalized.

"You foolish boy!" she scolded. "Now we have lost two valuable things. All that remains are these ten muskrat pelts. Take them to the village, Tabulech, and sell them for wampum, or the Chief will take our wigwam from over our very heads."

Tabulech promised that this time he would avoid the usual path and have nothing to do with the old man. So he took a new way through the depths of the wood and had nearly reached the village when he heard the sound of music. Despite all he could do, his feet turned toward the sound and began to dance of their own accord. He danced and he danced and could not stop, not even when he had danced up to the old man who played on a broken flute.

"Stop, stop!" pleaded Tabulech. "Stop playing!" and he threw the muskrat skins at the old man's feet.

The old man stopped playing, handed Tabulech the flute, and laughed till the tears ran down his cheeks.

"All right, my son," he said. "Go home now, and cheer up. You may have made better bargains than you know."

But the mother of Tabulech did not think so.

"A morsel of food," she wailed, "a shabby old belt, and a broken flute—for all those fine skins. And see, here comes the Chief for the tribute!"

It was so. The Chief, with a band of his braves, approached the wigwam. With a worried heart, but the customary Indian politeness, Tabulech invited the Chief to enter the lodge and showed him to the highest place. Having no other food, he offered the Chief the dish of food he had got from the old man. The guest looked disdainful, but tasted it, and then his expression changed. Never had he tasted anything so good! He ate and he ate, and the more he ate, the more there was. But the trouble was, he could not stop eating, even when his stomach began to hurt dreadfully.

"Take it away, or I shall die," he groaned, and Tabulech laughed. He knew just how the Chief felt.

"I shall take it away," he said boldly, "only when you promise that henceforth you will demand no tribute wampum, from me, or from any of the people!"

The Chief was terribly angry, but he was also in pain. He knew if he ate one more bite he would choke to death. So he gasped out, "Yes, yes! Anything you say!"

But as soon as Tabulech had removed the dish, he shouted to his braves:

"Seize this fellow and kill him!"

As the braves rushed forward, Tabulech threw down the magic belt and, quick as a striking snake, it jumped up and wound itself about the lot of them, and not one could stir a muscle. Then the Chief saw he was dealing with trickery, and cast about in his mind for a better trick.

"Let my men go," he said, "and we will make a bargain."

"Tell me what it is first," said Tabulech suspiciously.

"I have a daughter," said the Chief, "who never smiles, much less laughs. A spell was put upon her by Lox when she was a child." He looked at Tabulech with a sly grin. "If you can cause her to laugh, I will make you my son-in-law, and you and your mother will never know want again. If you fail, however, you will die!"

Tabulech thought for a moment, then bravely agreed to the bargain. And the Chief laughed to himself, for he knew

his daughter and he was sure that Tabulech would fail, and he would be rid of him.

Tabulech loosed the braves and accompanied the Chief to the village. There, before all the assembled people, the Malicete presented his gloomy daughter to Tabulech. She might have been a pretty maid had not her face stretched from here to here with sulky disdain.

Sitting at her feet, Tabulech began to tell a very funny story about an ant and a beaver, and the people laughed heartily, all but the Chief's daughter. She just sighed and looked gloomier than ever. So Tabulech told another tale, even funnier than the first. All the people fairly shouted with laughter, but not the tiniest smile appeared on the face

of the Chief's daughter. In desperation, Tabulech tried standing on his head and making funny faces, but nothing was any good. He had failed.

"I should have been glad if you had succeeded," the Chief said sourly, "for a gloomy face makes a dreary wigwam. However, you have failed and must pay the penalty." And he gave his braves the signal to kill Tabulech. As the braves advanced upon him, Tabulech snatched up the flute and began to play. At once the braves began to dance merrily, and not only the braves, but the Chief himself and all the people except the Chief's daughter, who still sat wrapped in gloom.

How they danced! They jigged and they whirled and they bobbed and they bounced! Fat and thin, short and tall, they all skipped about, and though they gasped for breath and wept with anger, they could not stop. They were a very funny sight indeed.

Suddenly a sound was heard above the music. It was the sound of laughter. Tabulech left off playing and stared at the Chief's daughter. She was laughing! She was laughing so hard, she rocked back and forth and the tears ran down her cheeks. When the music ceased and all collapsed on the ground, she laughed harder than ever.

"Take her!" gasped the Chief. "You have won. It is clear that you are a magician, and your magic is stronger than mine."

The people thought so too, for they made Tabulech their

Chief instead, and since the old Chief's daughter was now as cheerful as the summer sun, Tabulech married her and they had many children.

Only one thing puzzled Tabulech. Why, when he played the flute, had the Chief's daughter not danced too? But then, you see, he didn't know of Glooscap's part in the affair, and Glooscap really *is* a great magician!

Kespeadooksit—the story ends.

Mooin, the Bear's Child

NOW IN THE Old Time there lived a boy called Sigo, whose father had died when he was a baby. Sigo was too young to hunt and provide food for the wigwam, so his mother was obliged to take another husband, a jealous spiteful man who soon came to dislike his small stepson, for he thought the mother cared more for the child than for himself. He thought of a plan to be rid of the boy.

"Wife," said he, "it is time the boy learned something of the forest. I will take him with me today, hunting."

"Oh no!" cried his wife. "Sigo is far too young!"

But the husband snatched the boy and took him into the forest, while the mother wept, for she knew her husband's jealous heart.

The stepfather knew of a cave deep in the forest, a deep

cave that led into a rocky hill. To this cave, he led his stepson and told him to go inside and hunt for the tracks of rabbit. The boy hung back.

"It is dark in there. I am afraid."

"Afraid!" scoffed the man. "A fine hunter you'll make," and he pushed the boy roughly into the cave. "Stay in there until I tell you to come out."

Then the stepfather took a pole and thrust it under a huge boulder so that it tumbled over and covered the mouth of the cave completely. He knew well there was no other opening. The boy was shut in for good and would soon die of starvation.

The stepfather left the place, intending to tell the boy's mother that her son had been disobedient, had run off and got lost, and he had been unable to find him. He would not return home at once. He would let time pass, as if he had been looking for the boy. Another idea occurred to him. He would spend the time on Blomidon's beach and collect some of Glooscap's purple stones to take as a peace offering to his wife. She might suspect, but nothing could be proved, and nobody would ever know what had happened.

Nobody? There was one who knew already. Glooscap the Great Chief was well aware of what had happened and he was angry, very angry. He struck his great spear into the red stone of Blomidon and the cliff split. Earth and stones tumbled down, down, down to the beach, burying the wicked stepfather and killing him instantly.

Then Glooscap called upon a faithful servant, Porcupine, and told him what he was to do.

In the dark cave in the hillside, Sigo cried out his loneliness and fear. He was only six after all, and he wanted his mother. Suddenly he heard a voice.

"Sigo! Come this way."

He saw two glowing eyes and went towards them, trembling. The eyes grew bigger and brighter and at last he could see they belonged to an old porcupine.

"Don't cry any more, my son," said Porcupine. "I am here to help you," and the boy was afraid no longer. He watched as Porcupine went to the cave entrance and tried to push away the stone, but the stone was too heavy. Porcupine put his lips to the crack of light between boulder and hillside and called out:

"Friends of Glooscap! Come around, all of you!"

The animals and birds heard him and came—Wolf, Raccoon, Caribou, Turtle, Possum, Rabbit, and Squirrel, and birds of all kinds from Turkey to Hummingbird.

"A boy has been left here to die," called the old Porcupine from inside the cave. "I am not strong enough to move the rock. Help us or we are lost."

The animals called back that they would try. First Raccoon marched up and tried to wrap his arms around the stone, but they were much too short. Then Fox came and bit and scratched at the boulder, but he only made his lips bleed. Then Caribou stepped up and, thrusting her long antlers into the crack, she tried to pry the stone loose, but only broke off one of her antlers. It was no use. In the end, all gave up. They could not move the stone.

"Kwah-ee," a new voice spoke. "What is going on?" They turned and saw Mooinskw, which means she-bear, who had come quietly out of the woods. Some of the smaller animals were frightened and hid, but the others told Mooinskw what had happened. She promptly embraced the boulder in the cave's mouth and heaved with all her great strength. With a rumble and a crash, the stone rolled over. Then out came Sigo and Porcupine, joyfully.

Porcupine thanked the animals for their help and said, "Now I must find someone to take care of this boy and bring him up. My food is not the best for him. Perhaps there is someone here whose diet will suit him better. The boy is hungry—who will bring him food?"

All scattered at once in search of food. Robin was the first to return, and he laid down worms before the boy, but Sigo could not eat them. Beaver came next, with bark, but the boy shook his head. Others brought seeds and insects, but Sigo, hungry as he was, could not touch any of them, At last came Mooinskw and held out a flat cake made of blueberries. The boy seized it eagerly and ate.

"Oh, how good it is," he cried. And Porcupine nodded wisely.

"From now on," he said, "Mooinskw will be this boy's foster mother."

So Sigo went to live with the bears. Besides the mother bear, there were two boy cubs and a girl cub. All were pleased to have a new brother and they soon taught Sigo all their tricks and all the secrets of the forest, and Sigo was happy with his new-found family. Gradually, he forgot his old life. Even the face of his mother grew dim in memory and, walking often on all fours as the bears did, he almost began to think he *was* a bear.

One spring when Sigo was ten, the bears went fishing for smelts. Mooinskw walked into the water, seated herself on her haunches and commenced seizing the smelts and tossing them out on the bank to the children. All were enjoying themselves greatly when suddenly Mooinskw plunged to the shore, crying, "Come children, hurry!" She had caught the scent of man. "Run for your lives!"

As they ran, she stayed behind them, guarding them, until at last they were safe at home.

"What animal was that, Mother?" asked Sigo.

"That was a hunter," said his foster-mother, "a human like yourself, who kills bears for food." And she warned them all to be very watchful from now on. "You must always run from the sight or scent of a hunter."

Not long afterwards, the bear family went with other bear families to pick blueberries for the winter. The small ones soon tired of picking and the oldest cub had a sudden mischievous thought.

"Chase me towards the crowd," he told Sigo, "just as men do when they hunt bears. The others will be frightened and run away. Then we can have all the berries for ourselves."

So Sigo began to chase his brothers towards the other bears, whooping loudly, and the bears at once scattered in all directions. All, that is, except the mother bear who recognized the voice of her adopted son.

"Offspring of Lox!" she cried. "What mischief are you up to now?" And she rounded up the children and spanked them soundly, Sigo too.

So the sun crossed the sky each day and the days grew shorter. At last the mother bear led her family to their winter quarters in a large hollow tree. For half the winter they were happy and safe, with plenty of blueberry cakes to keep them from being hungry. Then, one sad day, the hunters found the tree.

Seeing the scratches on its trunk, they guessed that bears were inside, and they prepared to smoke them out into the open.

Mooinskw knew well enough what was about to happen and that not all would escape.

"I must go out first," she said, "and attract the man's attention, while you two cubs jump out and run away. Then you, Sigo, show yourself and plead for your little sister. Perhaps they will spare her for your sake."

And thus it happened, just as the brave and loving mother bear had said. As soon as she climbed down from the tree, the Indians shot her dead, but the two male cubs had time to escape. Then Sigo rushed out, crying:

"I am a human, like you. Spare the she-cub, my adopted sister."

The amazed Indians put down their arrows and spears and, when they had heard Sigo's story, they gladly spared the little she-bear and were sorry they had killed Mooinskw who had been so good to an Indian child.

Sigo wept over the body of his foster mother and made a solemn vow.

"I shall be called Mooin, the bear's son, from this day forwards. And when I am grown, and a hunter, never will I kill a mother bear, or bear children!"

And Mooin never did.

With his foster sister, he returned to his old village, to the great joy of his Indian mother, who cared tenderly for the she-cub until she was old enough to care for herself.

And ever since then, when Indians see smoke rising from a hollow tree, they know a mother bear is in there cooking food for her children, and they leave that tree alone.

Thus, kespeadooksit—the story ends.

Badger and the Star Wives

One day Badger and his brother were sunning themselves in a meadow when along came two flighty girls of the Micmac tribe. They had been sent to pick blueberries but, idling their time away in talk, they had little to show for their morning's work. Badger saluted the girls and asked what luck they were having.

"None at all," said the elder sister, preferring the stranger to think the fault lay in the scarcity of berries and not in themselves.

"You're not looking in the right place," said Badger, hiding a grin. "You should follow the sun to its going-down place. There you will find more blueberries than you ever imagined."

"Quick!" cried the younger girl, who was even more

foolish and impetuous than her sister. "Let us find them before someone else does," and away they went.

How Badger laughed, and Little Brother too.

"When they find the sun's going-down place," he told Little Brother, "it will be too dark to see blueberries or anything else!"

The two foolish girls followed the sun all afternoon and when it dipped below the treetops, they looked for berries. In the dusk, of course, they could hardly see anything, and not a berry could they find. Then, at last, they realized how they had been fooled and knew they must build a lodge where they were for the night, since it was too dark to travel.

Luckily, even very young girls are taught in the Wabanaki land how to build a wigwam, for amongst the Indians that is a woman's work. The sisters stripped young birches of their boughs and thrust them into the ground to form a cone. Then they laid birchbark over the cone and laid poles on the outside to hold the bark in position. Finally, they made beds of thick spruce boughs and lay down with their heads to the door, so they could look out at the sky.

"If you could marry a star," asked the younger girl sleepily, "which one would you choose? That large bright star or the small twinkling one?"

The elder girl yawned.

"The large bright one," she murmured, and fell asleep.

"I should like the little one," said her sister, and then she too drifted into slumber.

In the morning, the elder sister was first awake, and cried out with surprise at the sight of a young man with large lustrous eyes, standing within the wigwam.

"You wished for me," he said, "and here I am."

Beside him stood an older, smaller man, who looked at the other girl with little twinkling eyes.

"We are tired of living alone," he said.

Now the two astonished Indian maids did not remember their idle wishes of the night before, but they understood the men wished to marry them. They thought the men looked kind and that it would be very nice to have husbands to love and care for them, so they agreed to go and live with the men in their own country.

"Turn around three times," said the younger man, "with your eyes tightly closed." The girls did so, and on opening them, discovered they were in a strange new land. It was wide and open, without trees or water, and with a blue haze over everything. The girls thought it beautiful and settled down happily with their husbands in one large wigwam. The men were kind to them and gave them all they wanted, but warned them never to look under a certain flat stone which stood near the wigwam. Now, of course, this immediately aroused the girls' curiosity. Time after time, they looked at the stone and asked each other "What can be under it?" and "Why can't we look?"

At last, one day when their husbands were off hunting, the younger sister could bear it no longer.

"I must take just a tiny peep," she said, and lifted the stone.

To the sisters' amazement, they found themselves staring through a peephole at the earth itself! As if they were eagles, they could look down on green forests and lakes and rivers, their own land! Now at last they knew where they were—in the sky, with stars for husbands. At once they were homesick.

That night, when the husbands came home, they saw that the girls had been crying and guessed the reason. As they feared, the earth women now longed to return to their own people.

"Very well," said the star men sadly. "If you wish to go, we will show you the way."

"Go to sleep," said the younger man, "and when you wake, you will find yourselves where you were when you first wished for star husbands."

"Wait till you hear the chickadee sing," said the older man, "but do not open your eyes. Wait till the red squirrel sings, but even then, do not open your eyes. Wait till you hear the gray phoebe sing—then you may open your eyes."

The star wives slept for a long time, until at last they began to hear the familiar sounds of the forest. With closed eyes, they heard the chickadee sing. "Don't move," whispered the elder sister. Then the red squirrel sang. And the younger girl could wait no longer. Eagerly, she threw off her blanket.

"No, no!" cried her sister. "Wait till the gray phoebe sings!" But the younger star wife had already opened her eyes.

The star wives were no longer in the sky, but not on the ground either. They were on the topmost branch of a pine tree, halfway up to Sky and halfway down to earth, because they had not waited. Moreover, for their disobedience, they had been turned into weasels.

The elder girl wished very much to scold her younger sister for her impatience, but she knew that would not help. They must get down to the ground.

"There is Team the Moose," said she. "Let us ask for his help."

"Team, Team!" cried the younger sister. "Help us!"

"What will you give me if I do?" asked Team.

"Anything! You may even choose one of us to marry."

But Team shook his head disdainfully.

"No, thank you. I'm married already," and he passed on.

Next came Mooin the Bear.

"Oh, Mooin, save us and one of us will marry you!"

"I was married in the spring," said Mooin and passed on. Then came Abistanooch the Marten, and he just laughed at them. "I don't fancy marrying a weasel," he said. "I shall choose a mate from my own kind," and he, too, passed on.

"We ought to have stayed with our star husbands," moaned the elder sister. "We have been very foolish."

"Yes," said the younger, who was also learning wisdom.

"It is better to live in the Sky than in a tree."

"Look!" cried the first one. "There is the rascal who tricked us in the first place!"

Sure enough, it was Badger, looking up at them with a mocking grin. However, he did not recognize the girls he had fooled. To him they looked like ordinary weasels.

"What will you give me," he asked, "if I help you down?"

The girls said they had only themselves to give, and Badger said that was just what he wanted. What he had in mind, though, was two *roasted* weasels, not live ones—one for himself and one for Little Brother.

"Tie your hairstring around the branches," the elder star wife whispered, not trusting Badger this time. "I shall do the same with mine." Indian women wear strings of thin rawhide to bind their hair, and even though the girls were now weasels they still had their hairstrings.

Badger carried the elder sister down first, and she told him that after he had brought her sister down, he must go up the tree again and bring down the hairstrings which were very valuable and had magic in them. "Meanwhile," she said, "my sister and I will prepare the wigwam for you."

Badger willingly went up the tree since, if those hairstrings were valuable, he wanted them for himself. But they were tied in many hard knots, and it took him a long time to get them free. While he was busy at this, the sisters were busy building and furnishing the wigwam.

At last, hearing Badger descend, they crept out the back way and ran for their lives.

"The fun is over," cried Badger, drawing his knife. "Now for a good dinner of young weasel," and he strode into the wigwam. "Ouch!" he cried, as sharp thorns ran through his moccasins, and "Help!" he shouted as he bumped into a hornet's nest and the angry insects stung his face. "Oh, oh, oh!" moaned Badger as he stumbled over an anthill and the ants ran over him and bit him. The girls had prepared the wigwam well!

Now by the time Badger had escaped from the wasps and the ants and washed his stinging body in the brook, he was a very angry Indian indeed. He made up his mind that no matter what happened, he would find those weasels and punish them, and it was a simple matter to discover their track through the forest.

Meanwhile the two star wives, out of breath, had arrived at a broad river, too wide and too deep for two weasels to swim. Knowing Badger would soon be after them, they were very frightened and stared longingly at the other side. A croaking voice spoke behind them.

"Do you wish me to fly you across the river?"

It was Tumgwoligunech the Crane, and the girls joyfully accepted his offer.

"Hop on," he said, and away they flew across the water.

As he set them down on the far side, however, the crane spoke in a different voice—a deep and musical voice full of wisdom and authority.

"Would you indeed like to be star wives again and live in the Sky?"

The star wives were dumbfounded. How did he know?

"Sometimes men call me the Trickster," said the crane with meaning, and then the girls knew it was Glooscap.

"Oh yes, Master," they cried. "If our husbands will have us back, we would very much like to live again in the sky. We don't like being weasels at all!"

"Very well," said Glooscap, and he told them to turn around three times with their eyes tightly closed, until they heard the voices of their husbands. The weasels did so, obeying his instructions, and only opened their eyes when they heard their husbands crying, "Welcome home!" And if you look carefully at the night sky in midsummer, you may see four small stars around a piece of sky the shape of a wigwam. They are the two sisters and their husbands shining happily up there to this day.

Back on earth, Glooscap flew back across the river to deal with Badger. Presently the mischief-maker came running out of the woods.

"Here, you Tumgwoligunech," he shouted, "have you seen two weasels pass this way?"

"I just carried them over to the far side," said Glooscap in the crane's hoarse voice.

"Then take me over too!" demanded Badger. "And be quick about it."

The crane, however, was in no hurry. He smirked and fluffed up his feathers proudly. "Tell me," he said, "do I not have lovely smooth feathers?"

"Smooth—and dusty!" mocked Badger.

"But have I not a long, straight neck?"

"Very long," laughed Badger, "and no straighter than this winding river."

"Confess at least," the crane pleaded, "that my legs are very long and red."

"Oh, bother!" cried Badger, losing patience. "As long as your tongue, you old chatterer. Take me across!" And he jumped on the crane's neck.

Saying no more, the crane launched himself into the air

and flew with Badger high over the river until, half way across, he gave himself a shake.

"Help!" cried Badger, as he tumbled off and fell down, down, down into the water with a tremendous splash.

Glooscap watched Badger struggle with all his might to gain the shore. At last—wet, tired and breathless—Badger dragged himself from the water. Then he looked up—and waved.

"Thanks!" he shouted with a weak grin. "Just what I wanted—a refreshing swim!"

And Glooscap smiled. For he loved an indomitable spirit and, for all Badger's faults, he never gave in!

Now again, kespeadooksit—the story ends.

The Man Who Was Made a Magician

LONG AGO, in the days of Glooscap, there lived a boy named Widjek who could never do anything properly. Perhaps this was because people laughed at him. Nobody disliked Widjek, for he was gentle and friendly, but his awkwardness was funny and so they laughed. The more Widjek tried to win their respect, the more funny he seemed, and the more they laughed, the harder it was for poor Widjek to do anything right.

So, even when he became a man, he was as awkward as ever. He would keep dropping things and falling over his own feet. The people called him Widjek the Moonstruck, because they said he must once have slept with the moon's rays on his face and so spoiled his wits; but Widjek himself was sure he was just like other men except that people didn't laugh at *them*.

One day Widjek asked his grandmother to make an evening visit. To "make an evening visit" means in the Wabanaki to arrange a marriage. Now the grandmother knew it would not be easy to find a bride for Widjek, but she loved him and determined to do her best. She went first to the Chief's wigwam.

"My grandson is tired of living alone," she said timidly. The Chief smiled but shook his head.

Then she went to each lodge in turn, without success, until she came to the last one of all, which belonged to a man named Nokum who had three unmarried daughters.

"Which of you, my daughters," laughed Nokum, "wishes to marry Widjek the Moonstruck?"

The two older girls indignantly refused, but the youngest daughter, Masusi, who was a kindhearted girl, looked troubled.

"The poor fellow must have someone to care for him and keep his lodge," she said. "I will marry him."

Nokum scowled. He did not like this at all, for Masusi was his favorite daughter, and he hoped to marry her to someone better.

"If your grandson will provide all the meat for my lodge for a full year," he told Widjek's grandmother, "I shall accept him as my son-in-law." Nokum was pretty sure, you see, that the young man would fail.

However, Widjek was so happy to hear Masusi would have him as a husband that he set out next day, determined to show he could be a good provider. But it was the same old story. He could find little game, and even when he did, he stalked it so clumsily that his prey was off and away before he came within arrowshot. Poor Widjek hunted until dusk and got nothing.

Tired and discouraged, he started back to camp, wondering how he was to tell Masusi he had failed again.

Suddenly, he heard music. It was such beautiful music he stopped in his tracks, utterly bewitched. Then, in the path in front of him, appeared three small hairy men playing flutes. They were Megumoowesoos, the Little People of the forest, who are great magicians. Though they were only half as tall as himself, Widjek was so surprised to see them, he tumbled head over heels backwards. He had never met any Megumoowesoos before. However, they spoke to him in a friendly way and led him into their cave through a door cut out of the solid rock. There they offered him food and drink, and invited him to stay the night.

It was growing dark now and Widjek was glad to delay his return to camp empty-handed, so he accepted the invitation and enjoyed a good meal and a refreshing sleep. In the morning, when the Little People led him from the cave, he saw a great heap of venison lying on the ground.

"It is yours," said the chief Megumoowesoo. "Take it and if you need more, come back—but tell no one where you have been or who gave you these things."

Thanking them joyfully, Widjek hurried back to camp

with the bundle on his back. Now his future was sure! With the help of the friendly Megumoowesoos, he could easily keep Nokum's wigwam supplied with meat for a year.

When Widjek walked triumphantly into the village, the people stared at him strangely and his grandmother came running to him with tears in her eyes.

"Grandson!" she cried. "Why have you been gone so long? It is a whole year since you went away. We thought you dead."

Widjek was amazed, for it seemed to him he had been gone only a night and a day.

"It was the magic of the Megumoowesoos," he exclaimed and, forgetting the Little People's warning, he related all that had happened. The people listened with awe, but when he opened his bundle to show them the venison, they burst out laughing. Inside, there was nothing but a heap of poplar bark.

"It is clear," said Nokum coldly, "that you have deceived us. All year you have been ashamed to come home without meat, and now you think to fool us with this made-up story."

"It is all true!" protested poor Widjek. "I could show you the path I took, and the cave, and the footprints of the Megumoowesoos outside!"

The people laughed scornfully.

"Widjek the Moonstruck!"

But the Chief called for silence.

"Poplar bark," he said, "is the food of beavers. It may be that where he found this bark, we will find good beaver hunting."

Widjek gladly offered to lead the hunters to the spot, and he had no difficulty finding the path. It led straight to the place where he had met the Megumoowesoos. Widjek rushed to the end of the path and stared around in dismay. There was no cave now—no door—only bare rock! Moreover, there were no tracks, and no sign of poplar bark or beaver.

"This settles it," said Nokum. "You have had the year granted you, and have failed." Then all went back to camp, angry with the moonstruck one for disappointing them.

Poor Widjek lingered in the forest, ashamed to follow them. If only he had kept quiet about the Little People. Now his people would laugh at him more than ever. Perhaps even Masusi!

"Oh, why is it," he groaned, "why is it everything I do turns out badly? Am I indeed moonstruck?"

"Certainly not!" growled a strange voice, and Widjek jumped and looked behind him. There, coming down the path towards him, was the largest bear he had ever seen!

Widjek was no coward, but he had left his weapons some distance away and was helpless. He could never tackle such a creature with his bare hands! So he turned to run—and as usual in his excitement and nervousness, he tripped over his own feet and would have gone sprawling had not the

bear stretched out a paw to steady him.

"Fear not, Widjek," said the bear, "for I am he who made your ancestors from the ash tree."

Then Widjek knew he was in the presence of Glooscap.

"O Master," he cried, "I am not worthy of my ancestors. I try and I try to do things right, but I always fail."

"Never mind," said Glooscap, "you will do better in the future, if you will do as I tell you."

"Oh, I will!" cried Widjek eagerly.

Then Glooscap gave him a long curved horn.

"Put this to your ear, and you will hear animals talking a long way off. Follow the sound of their voices and you will always find game."

"They will hear me coming and run away," said Widjek sorrowfully. "They always do."

Then Glooscap gave him also a bag of white feathers and told him to burn them when he was drawing close to game.

"The smoke will be carried on the breeze to them, and they will fall asleep," said Glooscap. "Kill no more than you need for food and these magical powers will never fail you. Hereafter you will be known not as Widjek the Moonstruck, but as Widjek the Magician."

And before the young Indian could utter a word of thanks, the great bear had slowly dissolved into space.

This time Widjek kept his own counsel. He was learning wisdom at last.

He went hunting the very next day and quickly found

game by listening through the horn. Then he put the animals to sleep with the smoke from the burning feathers. When he returned to camp with a great load of venison—enough for Nokum's family as well as his own—the people were astonished.

On each succeeding day, he returned with meat enough for both wigwams. Then the people knew he must have some secret power.

"He has become a magician," they whispered to each other, and from that time on, they called him Widjek the Magician.

Now Widjek was a great and honored member of his tribe, and all the young maidens of the village, including the daughters of the Chief, wished to have him for a husband. The Chief called all the maidens together and told Widjek he could have any one he chose for a wife.

The young man walked slowly down the line of girls, looking carefully at each, and at last he came to Masusi—Masusi, who had chosen him when he was poor and lonely and despised.

"This is my bride," he said.

And far away on Blomidon, Glooscap nodded and puffed great smoke rings from his pipe. In his wisdom, he had known all the time that under Widjek's foolish appearance lay a brave and gentle heart. Now all the people knew it too, and would never laugh at him again.

And so—kespeadooksit, once again.

Rabbit Calls a Truce

In the long ago when Glooscap ruled over the Wabanaki, there lived two lively animals—Keoonik the Otter, and Ableegumooch the Rabbit, who were forever playing tricks on each other.

One day, when Keoonik was in swimming, Ableegumooch ran off with a string of eels he had left on the shore. Keoonik rushed out of the water and went in angry pursuit. He had no difficulty in tracking the rabbit, for the mark of the fish, touching the ground between jumps, clearly showed the way. He was astonished, however, when the trail ended at a clearing in the woods where a withered old woman sat by a small fire.

"Kwah-ee, Noogumee," said Keoonik, using the formal address for an elderly female. "Did you see a rabbit hopping this way, dragging a string of eels?"

"Rabbit? Rabbit?" muttered the old woman. "What kind of animal is that?"

The otter explained that it was a small brown jumping creature with long ears and a short tail.

"I saw no such animal," the old squaw grumbled, "but I'm glad you came along, for I'm cold and sick. Do please gather a little wood for my fire."

Obligingly, Keoonik went off to do so. Returning with the wood, he stared around in surprise. The old woman was gone. On the spot where she had sat, he saw the mark of a rabbit's haunches, and familiar paw-prints leading away into the woods. Then he remembered that Ableegumooch was very clever at changing his appearance and fooling people.

"Oh, that miserable rabbit!" cried Keoonik and set off again on the trail. This time the tracks led straight to a village of the Penobscot Indians, where Keoonik could see the rabbit in conversation with a thin sad man wearing the feather of a Chief in his hairstring. The wily otter cut himself a stout stick and waited behind a tree. Presently, Ableegumooch came strolling down the path, his face creased in an absent-minded frown.

Keoonik was ready for him. He brought the stick down on the rabbit's head with a thud, and Ableegumooch collapsed on the grass.

"That should teach him," thought Keoonik, with satisfaction, and he sat down to wait for the rabbit to recover.

Presently Ableegumooch came to his senses and staggered to his feet with a dazed expression.

"What did you do with my eels?" demanded Keoonik.

"I gave them to the Indians," muttered the rabbit, exploring the bump on his head with a groan.

"What did you do that for, you silly creature?"

"Those Penobscots are starving, Keoonik," said the rabbit. "For many moons someone has been stealing their food."

"Just the same," grumbled Keoonik, "those were *my* eels."

The rabbit thumped his hind legs on the ground with an air of great determination.

"Keoonik, we must find the robbers and punish them!"

"We?" asked Keeonik in astonishment.

"Yes, you and I," said his companion firmly. "Let there be a truce between us until we discover the thieves."

Keoonik thought to himself that Ableegumooch was a fine one to complain of people stealing other people's food! However, he too felt sorry for the Penobscots.

"All right," he agreed. "We'll have a truce," and they shook hands solemnly. Then they started back to the village to ask the Chief what they might do to help, but when they were still some way off they saw two other animals talking to him. These were Uskoos the Weasel and Abukcheech the Mouse, two animals so troublesome even their own families would have nothing to do with them.

"Let's listen," whispered Ableegumooch, drawing Keoonik behind a tree.

"We will find those robbers for you, Chief," they heard Uskoos say. "Don't you worry about a thing."

"You can depend on us," chimed in Abukcheech.

Ableegumooch nudged the otter.

"Did you hear that?"

"I heard," said Keoonik. "So the Indians don't need our help after all."

"I wonder," said the rabbit thoughtfully.

"What do you wonder? And why are we whispering?"

"Shhh! Let's think about it a little, Keoonik. Have you any idea how those two get their living? They sleep all day and go hunting only after dark."

"Some of us like to hunt after dark," Keoonik said fairly.

"Well, but listen," said the rabbit. "All the fur robes in the camp have been chewed and scratched and spoiled. What animals chew and scratch wherever they go?"

"Weasels and mice," answered Keoonik promptly. "Very well. Let's follow them and see what happens."

So Keoonik and Ableegumooch, keeping out of sight themselves, followed the weasel and the mouse a very long way, to a large burrow in the side of a hill where a number of other weasels and mice of bad reputation were gathered. All greeted Uskoos and Abukcheech and listened to what they had to say, while the rabbit and otter, hidden behind a blueberry bush, listened too.

"We were very sympathetic," smirked Uskoos, "and said we would help them."

"So now they won't suspect us," said Abukcheech, and all the mice and weasels chortled gleefully.

"It is time now," said Uskoos, "to call all the animals together and plan the conquest of the Penobscots. For we are smarter than the Indians and deserve to have all the food for ourselves."

"Very true!" all shouted.

"How will we get the rest to join us?" asked Abukcheech.

"The smaller ones will be afraid to say no to us," declared Uskoos. "We will use trickery on the others. We will tell them the Penobscots plan to destroy all the animals in the land, and we must unite in order to defend ourselves."

"Then, with Wolf and Bear and Moose to help us," cried Abukcheech, "we'll soon have all the Indians at our mercy!"

The otter and the rabbit could hardly believe their ears. Someone must warn the Indians.

"Come on," whispered Keoonik, but the rabbit only crouched where he was, tense and unmoving. The fact is, he wanted to sneeze! Ableegumooch wanted to sneeze more than he ever wanted to sneeze in his life before, but he *mustn't* sneeze—the sound would give them away. So he tried and he tried to hold that sneeze back. He pressed his upper lip, he grew red in the face, and his eyes watered—but nothing was any good.

"Ahhhhhh-ahhhhhh-choo!"

Instantly, the weasels and mice pounced on Keoonik and Ableegumooch and dragged them out of hiding.

"Spies!" growled Uskoos.

"Kill them, kill them!" screamed Abukcheech.

"I have a better plan," said Uskoos. "These two will be our first recruits." Then he told the prisoners they must become members of his band, or be killed.

Poor Ableegumooch. Poor Keoonik. They did not wish to die, yet they could never do as the thieves wished, for the Penobscots were their friends. Ableegumooch opened his mouth, meaning to defy the villains no matter what the consequences, and then his mouth snapped shut. He had heard a strange sound, the sound of a flute piping far away, and he knew what it was. It was the magic flute of Glooscap, and the Great Chief was sending him a message.

Into the rabbit's head popped the memory of something Glooscap had said to him once long ago, half in fun, half in earnest. "Ableegumooch," he seemed to hear the words again, "the best way to catch a snake is to think like a snake!" At once the rabbit understood. He set himself to think like the mice and the weasels, feeling the greed and selfishness that was in them. Then he had a plan.

"Very well," he said, "we will join you. Those Indians are certainly very cruel and dishonest. They deserve the worst that can happen to them. Why, only yesterday"—and here he gave Keoonik a secret nudge—"my friend and I saw them hide away a great store of food in a secret place. Didn't we, Keoonik?"

"Oh, yes, certainly," stammered Keoonik, wondering what trick the rabbit was up to now.

The weasels and mice jumped about in mad excitement. "Where? Where? Where is this place?"

"Take us there at once!" cried Uskoos, licking his lips.

"Certainly," said Ableegumooch, starting off towards the woods. "Just follow us."

Abukcheech the Mouse was right at their heels, but Uskoos soon shouldered him aside. Then each animal fought to be in front, and in this way all rushed through the forest, across the meadows, down into the valleys and over the hills, until at last—pushing and panting and grunting—they all reached the bottom of a grassy hill. Ableegumooch pointed to a pile of rocks at the top.

"You will find the wealth you seek up there," he cried. "Hurry, hurry! The best will go to those who get there first."

Away they all went, each struggling to be first. The rabbit and the otter stood aside and watched as the wild mob scrambled up the hill—up and up until suddenly, too late to stop, they found themselves teetering on the edge of a cliff, with nothing in front of them but space, and the sea far below. Those who were first tried to stop but were pushed over by those crowding behind—and so, screaming

with terror, down they all went, headlong into the sea.

"Well," said Keoonik, peering over the edge of the cliff with a shiver, "their tribes are well rid of them."

"So are the Penobscots," said the rabbit. "And now that together we have saved our friends from the mice and the weasels, Keoonik, let us go home together in peace as good neighbors should."

"I'm willing," said the otter, but he had no sooner taken a step than he sprawled on the ground. Ableegumooch had tripped him.

"That's for the knock on the head!" the rabbit laughed, and made for the woods.

Picking himself up furiously, Keoonik was after him, shouting, "Just wait till I catch you, I'll teach you to play tricks!" Their truce was over.

And Glooscap, looking down from Blomidon, laughed at their antics, for he knew that with all their mischief there was no greed or spite in the hearts of Keoonik and Ableegumooch, against the Indians or against each other.

Once more, kespeadooksit—the story ends.

Big Magwis and Little Magwis

LONG AGO, in a Wabanaki village, there lived two young braves, both with the name of Magwis. One was called Big Magwis, because he was big and rich and lived in a very large wigwam; the other was called Little Magwis, because he was poor and little and lived in a very small wigwam.

Now Big Magwis looked down on Little Magwis because he was a pauper. Yet in spite of having so much himself, he was still envious of what little his neighbor had. In particular, he was jealous of the small Indian's wigwam, which was very well made and stood in a shadier spot than his own. In the long hot days of summer, he hated his fine big lodge and looked with envy and greed at his neighbor's. If only there was some way he could have Little Magwis' wigwam as well as his own. Then, one day, he chuckled as he thought of a plan.

He strolled over to Little Magwis' wigwam and kicked idly at a large log which lay near the fire.

"Kwah-ee, my brother," said Big Magwis. "Tell me, could you jump over this log and land on both feet?"

"Certainly," said Little Magwis in surprise. "That would be easy."

"I bet you these two cakes of corn," said the larger Indian craftily, "that you can't do it and I can!"

Little Magwis smiled.

"That's a foolish bet, my friend. Look now—" and he jumped the log with the greatest of ease.

"Well, well," said Big Magwis, appearing crestfallen, as he handed over the cakes, "I didn't think you could do it, a little chap like you. But I tell you one thing, I bet you can't land on *one* foot across the river!"

Little Magwis looked at the wide river flowing alongside the camp.

"Of course I can't," he said. "Nobody could."

"I can," boasted Big Magwis and the smaller Indian looked at him with amazement. "Moreover," said Big Magwis, "I'll bet my wigwam against yours, with everything in them, that I can do it and you can't."

Little Magwis looked at the river again, measured the distance with his eyes, and said, "It's surely impossible, but I'm willing to try if you are."

"Very well," said Big Magwis with a sly grin. "You go first."

So Little Magwis ran very fast towards the river, took a flying leap off the bank and landed—splash—in the middle. As he swam slowly back to shore, he saw Big Magwis doubled over with laughter.

"It's all very well to laugh," said Little Magwis as he came ashore, "but now let's see you try it."

"Certainly," said the big fellow. "Watch me." And he jumped into his canoe and paddled rapidly across the river.

"Wait!" cried Little Magwis. "That's not right!"

But just then Big Magwis jumped out of his canoe, landing on one foot on the opposite shore.

"You see?" he shouted. "I bet you I could land on one foot, and I did! Nothing was said about *jumping* over! So now your wigwam and everything in it is mine!"

Poor Little Magwis. Tricked out of his home and all he owned, with nothing in the world but two small cakes of corn, he was so ashamed at being taken in by a foolish trick that he ran away from the village that same day.

At sunset, weary and hungry, he sat down under a tree and prepared to make a poor supper of the two small cakes of corn. A sound made him start to his feet. There stood an old Indian in a long brown cloak, eyeing his cakes hungrily.

"Oh dear," thought Little Magwis, "I haven't really enough for myself," but, being a kindhearted lad, he held out one cake saying, "You seem hungry, grandfather. Eat."

The old man thanked him and eagerly devoured the food.

"It is clear," sighed Little Magwis, "that he is much

hungrier than I am, and he is old." So he offered the old man the other cake.

Now I can tell you something the little Indian did not know. The old man was really Glooscap. And this was his way of testing Little Magwis, to see if he was the sort of person who deserved his help. He now saw that Little Magwis was an honest, generous-hearted lad, in spite of the trouble he had brought upon himself. So he said:

"Follow this path. Turn off to the right at the river, go on a little way, and you will see an oak tree under which the ground is dry and hard. When the evening star is seen in the sky, you must climb that tree and stay in it overnight. If you do as I say, you will have great good fortune." And before Little Magwis could open his mouth to ask any questions, suddenly the old man was not there any more!

Little Magwis guessed at once that this was big magic and resolved to do as the old man had said. He found the oak tree without difficulty and as soon as it was dark climbed up into its branches.

The ground underneath looked the sort of place used by travelers to camp overnight, for the earth was packed down hard. And sure enough, just as the moon rose, two booöins, or Indian wizards, came into the clearing and set up camp for the night. Little Magwis began to shiver and shake, knowing what would happen if he were discovered. Booöins would be sure to kill anyone who spied on them. Holding himself as still and small as possible, Little Magwis watched the boooins prepare their evening meal, and heard them talking to each other.

"You know that blind Chief in the village at the river's bend," said one.

"Yes," said the other, "what about him?"

The first one laughed in an ugly sort of way.

"How stupid those medicine men are! They are trying to cure his blindness with all sorts of remedies except the right one!"

The other booöin shouted so loud with laughter that Little Magwis nearly fell out of the tree.

"All he needs," said the first, "is a few drops of sweat from the hide of a white caribou."

When the two booöins had done laughing and eating, they fell asleep.

Little Magwis was still too frightened to move, so he stayed where he was, thinking how cruel the wizards were and how sad it was that the old Chief did not know their secret. He thought to himself that if he lived through the night and escaped the wrath of the booöins, he would give the blind Chief the proper remedy. Well, Little Magwis did live through the night without harm, though when the wizards awoke and went on their way, he was so stiff at first he could hardly move. He got down from the tree at last and set out for the village at the bend of the river.

There he learned that the wizards had spoken truth. The old Chief was blind and the medicine men had given up hope of curing him. Now when Little Magwis offered to restore the Chief's sight, the medicine men laughed in his face, but the Chief was desperate and willing to try anything.

"Help me," he said to the little Indian, "and I'll give you anything you ask."

"I will help you if I can," said Little Magwis, "but I want nothing in return. First, bring me a white caribou."

Today there are no caribou at all in the Maritime woodlands, only the deer, which were brought in some thirty or forty years ago, but in the Old Time they were very plentiful. However, the white ones were rare, and it was some time before one could be found and driven into the village. Little Magwis caught and held it by the antler while he wet his hairstring in the caribou's sweat. Then he squeezed the moisture into the Chief's sightless eyes.

After a long breathless moment, the Chief's staring eyes grew bright.

"I can see!" he cried. "I can see!"

Then all the people cheered, and the Chief ordered a large toboggan brought to him. He loaded it with venison and furs and fine weapons and decorated baskets, and gave it all to Little Magwis.

When Little Magwis arrived home in his own village with all these wonderful things, Big Magwis nearly choked with jealousy.

"How did you get it? Where—what—how?"

Little Magwis willingly told him the whole story.

"The oak by the camping ground?" cried Big Magwis. "I know it well!"

That night he stole off quietly and hid himself in the tree, hoping to overhear something that would bring him a fortune like his neighbor's. Crouched in the fork of the tree, hiding his big body as well as he could, he heard the booöins approach the spot underneath and listened eagerly to what they had to say.

"You remember our talk not long ago about the blind Chief?" asked one.

"I remember it well," said the other.

"I have just learned," said the first with a scowl, "that we were overheard by someone up in this tree—someone who got rich by curing the Chief with our secret remedy!"

"Perhaps," said the second in a hard voice, "perhaps he is up in that tree now, hoping to hear more of our secrets!" And he suddenly hurled a stone into the tree, knocking Big Magwis to the ground and killing him instantly.

Little Magwis never went to the tree again. He had more sense! And he was content with what he had.

There, once again—kespeadooksit.

The Magical Sweet-Grass Doll

In the Old Time there lived a Passamaquoddy Indian youth called Kayak, the youngest of seven sons. He was, in spite of his youth, the cleverest of the sons. He could swim better, shoot straighter, and fight harder than any of them. He seemed to do all things better than they, and this was because he first thought what he had to do, and then practiced until he could do it well.

His brothers were too lazy to go to all that trouble and, instead of admiring Kayak's energy, they were jealous of him and made his life miserable in any way they could. They even told false tales about him to his father. At last, the youth became so unhappy he decided to run away from home. Fearing his brothers might run after him and bring him back, he thought of a way to run faster than they could.

He shot an arrow into the air and ran after it, trying to catch it before it fell. He did this over and over, in secret, until he could outrun the arrow. At last, he could go like the wind.

It was time to set out, and Kayak made his secret preparations. His mother, the only one who loved him and who shared his secret, wished him good fortune and gave him a new pair of moccasins to wear on his journey. They were beautifully made of the finest doeskin, and Kayak wore them with pride. He embraced his mother and slipped away. Shooting his arrow and then outrunning it, he was soon far beyond pursuit.

Now Glooscap, the Great Chief, knew all about Kayak, and admired his wit and determination. However, he knew too that cleverness is not everything. Sometimes ambition is a hard and selfish thing. Did Kayak have a good heart? Was he honest? Was he kind? Glooscap determined to find out for himself.

Putting on the disguise of a poor old Indian, he came down from Blomidon and waited on the forest path. When he heard Kayak coming, Glooscap let a small box fall from his hand, as if he had dropped it accidentally, and walked on pretending to be old and weary and footsore.

Striding along cheerfully, Kayak saw the box on the path and picked it up. It was made of birchbark, decorated with porcupine quills, and it felt heavy. He was about to open it, when he caught sight of the old man on the path ahead.

For a moment the youth was tempted to keep the fine box for himself, but he knew that would be dishonest. So he ran after the old man, calling, "Kwah-ee, Grandfather!" Grandfather, in the Wabanaki language, is the polite word for "old man" and does not mean relationship. "Look! You have dropped something."

Glooscap took the box and said in an old man's quavering voice, "Thank you, my son. This contains something very precious, and I am grateful to you for finding it."

"It's lucky I came along," said Kayak cheerfully. "Can you tell me where this path leads, grandfather?"

"It goes a very long way," said the disguised Glooscap, "to a Micmac village on the edge of a lake called Kedgemakoogee"—and he sighed heavily—"yes, a very long way, and the path is full of rocks and thistles." He looked down at his feet, and Kayak looked too. Why, the poor old fellow had no moccasins! His feet were all cut and bleeding! In a moment, Kayak had pulled off his own moccasins and was putting them on the old man's feet.

"I am young," he said, as the old man protested. "I shall run so fast, I shan't feel the rocks and thistles," and he prepared to go on his way.

"Wait!" the old man said, and thrust the box into Kayak's hands. "This is yours now. I have no further use for it." And before Kayak could say thank-you, he was gone. Down the path? Up the path? Into the bushes? Kayak rubbed his eyes in amazement. The old man just was not there any more!

He looked at the box in his hand and lifted the cover, but what a disappointment. Inside, there was only a small doll, made of the sweet-smelling hay the Indians call sweet-grass, just such a doll as an Indian child would play with. Kayak shook his head ruefully.

"What shall I do with you, I wonder. I'm much too old to play with dolls."

To his astonishment, a voice at once replied.

"I am the servant of him who holds me in his hand. Whatever you ask of me, Master, that will I do."

The voice came from the doll! Kayak could hardly believe his ears. This was magic. Frightened suddenly, he put the doll back and closed the lid. He suspected now that the old man had been a magician, and you never can tell with magicians. Sometimes they play tricks on you. He would not use the doll's magic, he decided, unless he felt it absolutely necessary.

Late that day, Kayak arrived at the Indian village on the lake of Kedgemakoogee, and went into the first wigwam he saw. A kindly squaw gave him food and told him about the village and its people. They were of the tribe of Micmacs, also Glooscap's People, and their Chief was called Magooch.

Through the open door of the wigwam, Kayak saw a young maid pass, and cried out, "What maid is that? She is beautiful!"

"That is Seboosis," the old squaw replied, "the Chief's daughter."

Kayak turned eagerly to the old woman.

"Will you make an evening visit, Grandmother, and tell the Chief I am tired of living alone?"

Kayak was saying, you see, in the Indian fashion, that he wished her to ask for the girl in marriage. But the old woman shook her head doubtfully.

"I will go if you insist," she said, "but I fear Magooch means her to marry a man of our own tribe, a lazy useless fellow called Toobe."

"Try anyway," begged Kayak. "Go tonight!"

So the old woman went that evening to the Chief's wigwam and told him that Kayak was tired of living alone and wished to marry his daughter.

"Kayak?" growled Magooch impatiently. "Who is Kayak?"

She explained that he was the handsome stranger who had just come to the village. Curious to see the stranger, but making no promises, Magooch agreed to receive Kayak, and the youth shortly presented himself at the Chief's wigwam.

"Kwah-ee," he said politely and paused by the door, as a well-bred Indian should. You see, when a stranger enters an Indian home, he does not go to the honored place at the back of the wigwam unless he is invited. Usually the master of the house will say "Come up higher," or, in the case of a young man asking for a wife, if his suit is favorable, the master will say "Come up to the highest place, my son-in-law" and that means the marriage is made and the couple are man and wife.

The father of Seboosis said nothing.

He was thinking to himself that the young man looked too clever. He would rather have Toobe for a son-in-law, for

Toobe was timid and weak, and would always do as his father-in-law told him. However, an Indian does not like to say "No" straight out. He prefers to speak in a roundabout fashion which he considers more polite.

"There is a mountain out there," said Magooch to Kayak, "which stands in the way of our hunting grounds. I should like it removed."

Kayak understood, with a sinking heart, that the Chief was setting him an impossible task so that he would fail, and then he remembered the magical sweet-grass doll.

"I shall remove it for you," said he, "tonight!" And he left Magooch's wigwam. The Chief laughed to himself, but Seboosis was sad, for she had fallen in love with Kayak, and how could any man move a mountain?

When the red sun had disappeared behind the trees, Kayak went to the mountain and opened his birchbark box.

"Now, my magical sweet-grass doll," said he, "let us see what you are able to do. Remove that mountain before the rising of the sun!"

All through the night the puzzled Micmacs heard strange noises outside the camp, like giants digging, and huge rocks and trees crashing to the ground, but they were too afraid to go out to see what was happening. When at last the sun arose and all was still, they came out of their lodges and gasped with amazement. The mountain was gone!

Old Magooch was thunderstruck, and frightened too, for he saw that Kayak had great power. He feared that his people might transfer their respect from him to Kayak and make him Chief instead. Determined that Kayak must be got rid of, he called the youth to him and said:

"There is a tribe of Etamankiaks across the lake, who are our enemies. If you will lead a war party out and destroy them, you may marry my daughter."

Magooch knew that the Etamankiaks were very numerous and strong, yet he sent only a few braves to help Kayak, hoping all would be killed.

The young men were frightened and said to Kayak, "Stop! Let us go no farther. Magooch is sending us to our death!"

Kayak smiled as he fingered the sweet-grass doll hidden in his belt.

"Stay here," he said. "I shall go alone," and with the swiftness of the wind he was gone.

The men waited, and listened, and at last heard far off the sound of battle—the frightening sound of war whoops, the clash of arms, and dying screams. And—at last—silence.

"He was a brave man," the braves said soberly, and returned to camp to tell the Chief what had happened.

Secretly the Chief was well pleased, but he pretended to feel sorrow.

"He was indeed a great fighter," he said solemnly, "and gladly would I have received him as my son-in-law. However, now that he is dead, Seboosis will marry Toobe," and he ordered a wedding feast prepared.

Seboosis wept, but knew she must obey her father.

"Let the bridegroom come," called Magooch from his lodge, and Seboosis turned away to avoid the hateful sight of Toobe. She heard a voice say, "I am here, my father-in-law," and looked up with joy and amazement. There stood Kayak, alive and triumphant.

"The Etamankiaks are wiped out," said Kayak with meaning, and Magooch knew he must keep his promise. Hiding his rage and disappointment, he muttered, "Come to the highest place, son-in-law," and so Kayak and Seboosis were married and were very happy.

As for the magical sweet-grass doll, Kayak put it away in a safe place, saying to himself, "The doll has won me a wife and a home, and that is good. From now on I must do things for myself, or I shall grow fat and lazy." Kayak understood, you see, that there is more happiness in doing things for oneself than in depending on others.

And Glooscap, in his lodge on Blomidon, smoked his great pipe contentedly, rejoicing at Kayak's wisdom.

And so, kespeadooksit—the story ends.

Run, Rabbit, Run

IT WAS late winter or very early spring, for snow still lay on the ground, when Ableegumooch the Rabbit entertained two friends at a maple syrup feast. The two friends were Keoonik the Otter and Miko the Squirrel.

As they happily licked the last of the syrup off their paws, they exchanged news.

"Last night," said Miko, "the moon looked into my den and woke me, and I heard wolves talking outside. I heard them offer Lusifee the Wild Cat two strings of wampum to kill somebody!"

"Really?" asked the rabbit, with interest. "Who?"

"They didn't mention any name," said the squirrel, "but only spoke of him as a servant and friend of Glooscap, one full of tricks, who knows his way through the forest."

"Whoever he is," said Keoonik darkly, "he is as good as dead, for that Lusifee is a cunning tracker and absolutely cold-blooded."

"A friend of our Master's," mused Ableegumooch, "could be any of us."

"Someone full of tricks," remarked the otter uneasily. "It could even be me!"

"Hah!" snorted the rabbit, "you know very well that *I* am the one most full of tricks hereabouts." And Keoonik did not deny it, for he had suffered much in the past from the rabbit's mischief. Miko gave a little shiver.

"You know, when they spoke of one who knew his way through the forest, I couldn't help wondering if they meant me, for I can find my way through the trees better than most."

"Nonsense!" snapped Ableegumooch. "Anything a squirrel can do, a rabbit can do better. After all, *I* am Glooscap's official forest guide. And his very good friend," he added proudly.

"The thing is," said Keoonik, his eyes dwelling unconsciously on the rabbit, "to find someone who fits all three requirements—someone full of tricks, one who knows the forest, and one who is a servant and friend of the Great Chief."

The rabbit jumped as if a bee had stung him.

"Oh my! It's *me* he's after!"

Keoonik tried to comfort the stricken rabbit.

"We'll stand by you," he said. "Won't we, Miko?"

"Y-yes," said the squirrel doubtfully, for he feared that even the three of them together would be no match for the ferocious cat.

"Thanks, my friends," said Ableegumooch, heartened by their loyalty, "but I may not need your help. I have a plan."

Miko asked what he had in mind.

"Strength and speed are on Lusifee's side, so I must rely on craft," said Ableegumooch and grinned mysteriously. "When a rabbit's skin falls short, he must borrow another's. Well, he's sure to come here to find me. I'm off!" And the rabbit sprang into the air, landing a long distance from his lodge, so as to leave no track near his home. Ableegumooch kept jumping in this way until he thought he was out of scent and sight, then scampered away like the wind.

Keoonik and Miko scurried to a hiding place nearby and waited to see what would happen. Presently, sure enough, Lusifee the Wild Cat appeared, slinking along with nose to the earth, his yellow eyes gleaming and his great paws padding silently over the snow.

Finding the rabbit's wigwam empty, he snarled with disappointed fury. However, taking the wigwam for a center, he kept going round and round it, making each circle a little wider than the one before, until at last he found the rabbit's scent. He kept on circling until he reached the spot where the rabbit had stopped jumping. Then, swearing by his tail to catch Ableegumooch and kill him, he set out swiftly on a clear trail.

As the day passed, Lusifee knew by the freshness of the track that he was overtaking the rabbit, but he did not catch sight of his prey while daylight lasted. As night fell, Lusifee came upon a wigwam all alone on the open marsh, and he poked his head inside. There sat a grave and dignified old fox, whose white hair stuck up oddly on either side of his head. When asked if he had seen Ableegumooch, the old fellow shook his head, but invited Lusifee to pass the night with him.

"You can continue your search in the morning," he said in a helpful manner. So, being tired and hungry, Lusifee accepted the invitation, and after a good supper, lay down by the fire and slept soundly.

Towards morning, however, he began to shiver and feel most uncomfortable. Waking at last, he looked around in amazement. He was no longer in the warm lodge but lying on the open marsh with snow blowing over him. Then Lusifee saw dimly the marks of a rabbit's feet and knew Ableegumooch had fooled him. The rabbit, artful at disguise, had masqueraded as the fox and had removed himself and the wigwam while Lusifee slept.

Resuming the chase in a great rage, the cat swore by his teeth, as *well* as by his tail, that Ableegumooch would die before nightfall. But when darkness came again, he had still not caught sight of the rabbit.

Stopping at the first village he came to, which was that

of a porcupine tribe, he asked the first young porcupine he met if he had seen a rabbit pass this way.

"Hush!" said the porcupine. "Can't you see we are listening to the storyteller?" Then Lusifee noticed that the whole tribe was gathered around the fire listening to an old porcupine with white whiskers and oddly-shaped ears. In the land of the Wabanaki, the storyteller is greatly respected, and it is considered most impolite to interrupt him. So the cat was obliged to wait until the stories were over. Then he turned once more to the young porcupine.

"But *have* you seen a rabbit?"

"Hundreds of them," answered the other impatiently, "are racing about in the cedar swamp near here. You can have as many as you want."

"Those aren't the ones I'm after," complained the cat. "I want Ableegumooch, Glooscap's forest guide."

The young porcupine said he knew of no other sort of rabbit save the wild wood ones, but perhaps the storyteller who was old and wise could tell him something.

So Lusifee went to the storyteller and asked if he had seen a rabbit pass by.

"Rabbit?" The storyteller rattled his quills as he thought, and the cat moved back prudently. "No, I've seen no rabbit. But, my friend, you look tired. You may pass the night with me, if you like, in my lodge outside the village."

The cat was glad of the invitation and went to sleep in a warm bed. Much later, he awoke, all a-shake and a-shiver in a wet cedar swamp, the wind blowing ten times worse than the night before, and all around him the tracks of a rabbit.

Lusifee sprang up more enraged than ever and, swearing now by his claws, as *well* as by his teeth and his tail, to be revenged on the rabbit, he set out again on the trail. He ran all day and at night came to another village, inhabited by a tribe of bears. He was so weary he could only gasp out:

"Have—you—seen—a rab—bit?"

The bears said they had not, but invited him to join in a feast with them, and when they had done eating, they politely asked him for a song. Now the cat was very vain about his voice, and right willingly he lifted up his voice in a song of hate against rabbits. The bears applauded and invited him to join in the dancing, but the cat begged to be excused on account of weariness and sat to one side, watching.

Now one of the bears was smaller than the others and his ears were somewhat longer than bears' are usually. However, he was a great dancer and leaped higher in the air than any other. As he passed by Lusifee he accidentally, it seemed, gave the cat a fierce kick, cutting his head and knocking him senseless.

When the cat came back to consciousness, he found himself in a wigwam outside the village. A medicine man of the bear tribe was bending over him and the cat noticed that he wore long white feathers on either side of his head. By now Lusifee was growing more suspicious and he looked at the medicine man with narrowed eyes.

"I was asking if any rabbits had been around here," said Lusifee, "and truly you look very much like one yourself. How did you get that split lip?"

"Oh, that is very simple," said the medicine man, who was no other than Ableegumooch, of course. "Once I was hammering wampum beads, and the stone on which I beat them broke in halves and one piece flew up and split my lip."

"But why are the soles of your feet so yellow, like a rabbit's?"

"Simple, again," said the medicine man. "I was once preparing some tobacco and as I needed both hands to work, I held it down with my feet—so the tobacco stained them yellow."

Then Lusifee suspected no more and allowed the medicine man to doctor his cuts with salve, after which he fell asleep. But, alas, once more the unhappy cat awoke in dreadful misery, his head swollen and aching, his wound stuffed now with hemlock needles instead of salve.

Now Lusifee swore by his body and soul, as *well* as by his teeth and his claws and his tail, to kill the next thing he met, rabbit, or any other!

Forgetting pain and cold, he rushed off, exulting when he found the track of Ableegumooch very fresh. Evidently the rabbit too was tiring from the race and could not be far off. Yes, there was the tricky follow just ahead! In fact

Ableegumooch had been obliged to stop short as he came to the edge of a broad river. The cat grinned with triumph, for he knew that rabbits are no good at swimming.

"You can't escape me now," he shouted.

Poor Ableegumooch. He could run no further.

Far away on Blomidon's misty summit, Glooscap saw all that had happened and knew the rabbit had done all he could by himself. The Great Chief began to smoke his pipe very hard, puffing black rings into the blue sky, where they changed at once into birds.

Down in the forest, Ableegumooch had turned at bay and Lusifee was prepared to spring—when, suddenly, down from the sky hurled a great flock of giant hawks screaming their war cries. Lusifee snarled and turned to meet them, but they bore him down by force of numbers—picking at his eyes and beating him with their wings—until at last, screaming with fear, the cat turned tail and fled into the forest, where if he is not dead he is running still!

Trembling with fright, Ableegumooch sank down to rest at last. He was not half so cocky as he had been when he started out, for he knew that but for the hawks he would have been a dead rabbit. A flute was playing far off, and the rabbit listened. Then he knew who had sent the hawks to him in the nick of time.

"Thank you, Master," he whispered. Glooscap, far off on Blomidon, nodded—and played a triumphant tune to the returning birds.

Now, kespeadooksit—the story ends.

The Boy Who Worried Tomorrow

ONCE IN THE days of Glooscap there lived a happy-go-lucky Indian boy named Chebec, who was always getting into trouble because he rushed about with his head in the air, never looking where he was going. He would dash along, chasing a bird or a butterfly, never looking at the path in front of him, and fall splash into a brook! That was Chebec, always plunging ahead without thought. He just never looked ahead.

Why, there were times when he looked no further than his nose—like the day he blundered into a wasps' nest and the angry wasps chased him all the way home. However, in spite of all such adventures, Chebec somehow survived and grew up to be a man who was just as thoughtless. One fine day, he decided all on the instant to leave home.

"You have a good place here," his family argued. "You will be lonely without your own people."

Chebec laughed as he shouldered his bundle.

"Perhaps," he said, "but I'll worry about that tomorrow." And off he went.

On the first day of his journey, Chebec felt light and carefree, striding along in the warm sunlight wondering what adventures lay ahead. He slept that night in a warm wood, and dreamed happy dreams.

But on the following day, the woods thinned out and looked strange to him, and as the sun went down the air grew chill. On both sides of the path lay bogland, offering no resting place for the night.

Chebec began to feel very lonely and frightened, and thought longingly of his home and family. An owl hooted menacingly overhead, and for a moment Chebec was tempted to turn and run back the way he had come, but pride prevented him. He pressed on into the darkness with a quaking heart, until with a start of joy he saw lights ahead —a campfire!

Chebec dashed towards the light in his usual headlong fashion, not stopping to wonder if the people were friends or enemies. Fortunately, they were Penobscots like himself and made him welcome.

Chebec was happy again to be amongst friends, but as he ate the food brought to him, he grew conscious of something strange about the village. It seemed to him that an air of sadness hung over it. The people never smiled, and there were no children. This was strange, for Indians are fond of children and proud to be the fathers of many sons. There were few women about, and the ones he saw were mostly old. There was only one who was as young as himself, and this was the girl who waited on him and smiled at him shyly. Chebec thought her the prettiest girl he had ever seen. Indeed, her name Kaloosit, which means "pretty woman," described her exactly. By the time the meal was over, Chebec was head over heels in love with Kaloosit.

So, in his usual impulsive way, he rushed to the father of Kaloosit and said, "Sir, I am tired of living alone!"

Kaloosit's father shook his head.

"Nothing would please me more," he said mournfully, "than to have a son-in-law, for I grow old and wish grandchildren before I die. But no one can marry in this village." Then he told Chebec how, whenever a couple in the village were wed, a giant Chenoo came straightway and stole the bride, carrying her off to his cavern in a high cliff, around which a storm always raged, and where pointed rocks like the teeth of hungry foxes waited and glittered in the sea below. And nobody could kill the Chenoo, because he took care to keep his soul in a secret place.

By soul, you understand, the Wabanaki meant that mysterious power that makes men live. They thought of it as something that had shape and size and color, and believed that a man could not be killed if his soul, or seat of life, was not in his body. The soul of the evil Chenoo, it appeared, was kept in a locked box on top of a high mountain which no man could climb. Moreover, the key to that box was hidden in another box at the bottom of the sea.

However, Chebec could not be bothered worrying about such far-off things. All he wanted was to marry Kaloosit.

"With your permission," he said, "I shall marry your daughter tomorrow." And he closed his ears to all the older man's arguments. When Kaloosit added her persuasion and the girl's father saw that the two young people were determined to marry, he threw up his hands.

"Very well! But you will surely lose her."

"I'll worry about that tomorrow," said Chebec.

In the morning he presented himself at the door of the lodge, while all the people stood about watching.

"Come up to the highest place, my son-in-law," said the father of Kaloosit, and these words meant they were now man and wife. Yet, even as the old man spoke the words, there came a great rush of air into the wigwam, and a great roaring voice cried:

"A-hah! Another bride for me!"

And there in their midst stood the awful Chenoo, so tall his head touched the roof of the wigwam, so fierce that Chebec quailed before him, and so strong he picked Kaloosit up like a feather and carried her away to his cave to join his other brides. Now there was great weeping and wailing in the village.

"What did I tell you?" groaned Kaloosit's father. "Now you have lost your bride and I, my daughter."

"Never mind," said Chebec staunchly. "I shall go at once to the Chenoo's cave and bring her back."

"The Chenoo will kill you!" the people cried.

Chebec shrugged.

"I'll worry about that later," said he, and off he went.

Now, on his way to the giant's home, Chebec had to cross a small stream. Hearing a small voice wailing, he paused.

"Save me, save me," the voice cried.

Then Chebec saw a tiny fish caught in a tangle of twigs and stones at the edge of the brook.

"Get me out, get me out!" wailed the fish. "Put me back in the water or I shall die."

Chebec carefully moved away the twigs so as not to hurt the small creature, and finally managed to release it.

"Thank you, thank you," cried the small fish joyfully. "Take a scale from my back, and if ever you should need my help, warm it with your hand and I will gladly serve you."

Chebec smiled to himself, thinking it unlikely he'd ever need the help of a small fish. However, he did not care to hurt the creature's feelings, so he put the scale away in his belt and hurried on. He was still a long way from the Chenoo's cave when he heard a plaintive cry among the trees. He turned off the path and found a small caribou with its horns caught in the branches of a hawthorn tree.

"Please let me out of here," wailed the caribou. "I'm caught!"

It took Chebec some time to free the animal's antlers, and when he had done so, the caribou thanked him warmly. "Take a tuft of hair from my tail," he said, "and if ever you are in trouble, warm it in your hands and I will come." So Chebec took the hair and tucked it into his belt with the scale, and went on.

Soon he was delayed once again, this time by a small hawk caught in a rabbit snare.

"Dear me," sighed Chebec, "if it isn't one thing it's another," but he felt sorry for the bird and took time to release it.

"Many thanks," cried the hawk. "Now take a feather from my crest and when you are in trouble, warm it with your hand and I will come." Chebec thanked the hawk and hurried on.

Now at last, in the distance, Chebec saw the giant's home. The great cliff rose steeply out of the sea, and dark clouds hung over it. As Chebec drew close, a great storm began to rage about him. The wind shrieked and tore his hair, the rain lashed at him, and the sea's spray filled his mouth.

Chebec plunged bravely into the thick of the storm and began to climb the face of the cliff, looking for the opening to the Chenoo's cave. Wet and cold, buffeted by the wind, he scrambled all over the cliff, finding no hole or crevice larger than his hand. Chebec sank down at last on a ledge near the sea, in despair.

He heard, but scarcely noticed, the honking of a Canada Goose overhead. Then there was the beating of great wings and the goose fluttered down beside him. Chebec stared at it, amazed. This was certainly the largest goose he had ever seen, and it looked into his face without fear. Then the great goose spoke to Chebec in his own tongue.

"Chebec, my son, see what happens when you don't look ahead." And Chebec knew it was the voice of Glooscap.

"O Great Chief, that is true," cried poor Chebec, "but it is too late to think of that now. I must save my wife."

And Glooscap answered, "Since you have shown kindness to the caribou, the fish and the hawk, I will help you just this once." And suddenly a tomahawk appeared in the air before Chebec. He grasped it eagerly. "Use it to cut a door in the cliff. But before you use it—" Glooscap paused significantly, "stop and think a moment." Then with a whirr of his powerful wings, the Canada Goose flew off into the storm.

Now in his eagerness and haste, Chebec began to hack at once at the cliff, until suddenly he remembered Glooscap's last words. For the first time in his life, Chebec sat down quietly and thought things over. He would now be able to enter the giant's cave. However, once inside, how could he destroy the giant? He had no way of finding the giant's soul. He could not swim to the bottom of the sea. He could not climb that high mountain. Ah, but wait! What about the friends he had made on his journey?

Taking the scale, the hair and the feather from his belt,

Chebec warmed them in his hands, and at once the fish, the caribou and the hawk were beside him. Chebec explained his trouble.

At once, the fish swam off and found the Chenoo's box on the bottom of the ocean and brought it back. The caribou forced open the locked box with his horns, and there inside lay the key to the other box. The hawk flew off to the

high mountain which no man could climb, and brought back the box containing the Chenoo's soul. Chebec seized the key and turned it in the lock. Inside the box lay the Chenoo's soul in the shape of a giant pine cone!

Now Chebec took Glooscap's magic tomahawk and cut a door in the rock, crying out, "Kaloosit—come!"

The door flew open and out ran his bride, closely pursued by the giant. Chebec put his wife behind him and waited as the giant rushed toward him. Clutching the giant's soul in his hand, he trembled as he felt the giant's breath upon his face. He squeezed the cone with all his might and felt it grow smaller in his hand.

"Look," cried Kaloosit, "the Chenoo is shrinking!"

It was true. Just like the cone in Chebec's hand, the giant was growing smaller and smaller and smaller, until—

"Stop, stop!" moaned the Chenoo in a tiny voice. "Don't kill me. I can't harm you now."

Chebec dropped the cone. Joyfully, the little Chenoo picked it up and ran. And no one has ever seen him from that day to this.

When Chebec got back to the village with Kaloosit, and all the other lost brides as well, the people acclaimed him a hero and made him Chief of the tribe. And, in order to keep this high position, Chebec was obliged at last to think before he spoke, to look before he leaped, and always to look a little further than his nose!

Thus, kespeadooksit—the story ends.

Badger and the Koondao

BADGER was up to his tricks again.

He had met a stranger in the forest and invited him to camp with him overnight. As they sat by the fire, they smoked their pipes and told stories until it grew very late, so late that Badger could hardly keep from yawning. However, it was a matter of pride with him not to fall asleep. Besides, being such a deceiver himself, he was always suspicious of other people. He would feel safer when the unknown Indian was asleep. He thought of a trick.

"My friend," said he, "can you tell me what my backlog is?" meaning the log against which he was leaning.

"Hickory?" inquired the stranger.

"No, not hickory."

"Maple?"

"No, not maple."

"White oak?"

"No, not white oak."

And so it went on, the stranger mentioning moosewood, ash, pine, cedar, birch, and all the wood he could think of, while Badger kept on saying no it was not this, or that. Their voices rose and fell with such monotonous regularity that the man grew sleepier and sleepier, until at last he slumped down fast asleep. Annoyed at the man for being so long about it, Badger thought of another trick to play. He spread sticky clay over the sleeper's eyes and then quickly departed.

When the man awoke, he thought he was blind, and was in a terrible state until he discovered the clay and rubbed it off.

"If ever I meet with that fellow again," he vowed bitterly, "I'll crush him to bits!"

Now this man, as it happened, was a booöin, and such wizards are very unpleasant fellows. It would be well for Badger if he never crossed Koondao's path again. Koondao, which means "stone," was the wizard's name, and he could become a huge stone at will.

Meanwhile, Badger had returned to his own lodge and told Little Brother to prepare for a journey.

"We are going to see what is new in the world," he said, and as Little Brother was always willing to do what Badger said, away they both went.

They had not gone far when they met a very tall and handsome Indian, wearing a shining belt and a necklace of purple stones. Badger recognized the amethyst beads and knew at once it was Glooscap the Great Chief. He felt somewhat nervous, but when Badger is frightened he is always more impudent than ever.

"Kwah-ee, Master," he saluted the Chief jauntily.

"Badger," said Glooscap sternly, "some day, with those tricks of yours, you will go too far. If your mischief should be the death of you, what would become of Little Brother?"

"That's just what's been worrying me," said the troublemaker merrily. "And so, my Chief, I think you should give me a *teomul* to keep me from harm!" A *teomul,* you know, is Indian for "magic charm."

Glooscap was about to rebuke Badger for his impudence, but then he thought to himself that perhaps a reward might have more effect on the troublemaker than punishment. It was at least worth a trial.

"Very well," he agreed, touching his magic belt. "I give you a charmed backbone."

"Hurray!" cried Badger.

"But you may use its magic only once," warned the Great Chief. "Be sure you use it wisely." Then, as suddenly as he had appeared, Glooscap was gone.

"Hurray for my backbone," laughed Badger. "And now, Little Brother, let us find some fun."

"I'm hungry," said Little Brother.

"Very well. I'll take care of that."

And away they went through the forest. Presently, they met two young boys. Now these boys, though Badger did not know it, were of the Culloo tribe, the Culloos being magicians who could, when they wished, turn themselves into enormous birds. Badger greeted the boys and asked where they lived. The boys pointed across the river, and Badger began to admire their bows and arrows.

"Let me feel how stiff they are," he said, and when he had them in his hand, he bent them so sharply they broke in pieces. "Dear me," said Badger in mock dismay, "what a pity. However, down the river a way, there is a large grove of birch which makes the very best bows. Listen!" and he cocked his head as if he could hear sounds. "There are some of your friends now, cutting down the trees. Hurry, so you may get your share."

The boys could hear nothing but the wind in the trees and the birds singing, but they were anxious to have new bows, so they hurried off down the river, going farther and farther from home. Badger laughed and told Little Brother to hide himself under a spruce tree.

"I am going to pay a visit to their lodge and get some dinner," he said. He reached into his blanket and pulled out a fine shirt, a feathered headdress, and a string of shell beads. When he put them on, he looked as grand as a Chief, and when he presented himself at the lodge of the Culloo woman, she bowed deeply.

"What can I do for you, O Chief?" asked she.

"Call your two boys," said Badger imperiously, "for I have something of importance to say to them."

The mother thought this must mean some good fortune, so she hurried away into the trees, calling out to her sons to come home. As soon as her back was turned, Badger lifted the meat off the fire and made off with it—and he and Little Brother shared a fine meal.

Soon afterward, the mother returned with her boys and found her dinner gone. It was clear that a trick had been played on them.

"It is that same rascal who broke our bows and led us on a wild goose hunt down the river," said the boys. "Come, let us go after him and teach him a lesson!" And, turning themselves into birds, they flew off.

Badger saw them coming and told Little Brother to hide.

"I shall lead them a merry chase," cried he, and was off like the wind, so fast the young Culloos could not overtake him—except one, who came close enough to snatch at the beads around his neck and break them. As the beads streamed away in the wind, Badger laughed.

"Thank you! Those beads were heavy. Now I can run much faster!"

The young Culloos called for help from their uncle, Kakakooch the Crow. Kakakooch flew after Badger and just managed to seize his headdress.

"Oh, how good you are," the merry Badger laughed.

"You have done me a great favor. My head was growing very hot. Now I can run faster than ever."

Then Kakakooch called on Uncle Kitpou the Eagle, begging him to catch Badger and punish him. Uncle Kitpou could fly faster than the others, but even so he only managed to snatch off Badger's shirt.

"Oh, thank you, thank you," cried Badger, as he ran on. "I was just wishing to be rid of that heavy shirt."

It looked as though Badger would escape them all.

Then, suddenly, down out of the sky came the Culloo boys' father, the giant Culloo himself, the biggest and strongest bird in the whole sky. He caught Badger up in his claws, body and bones, carried him to a high cloud, and let go! Badger fell heels over head, and from such a height he fell all night, from dusk to dawn, and the Culloo followed him down.

"Hurrah for a race!" cried Badger. "Swish, swish!" And he flapped his arms like the Culloo, imitating the sound of his wings. However, when at last he neared the ground, even Badger grew worried. That ground looked very hard. Just at the last moment, he remembered to cry out, "Oh spare my backbone!" and the next instant he struck the earth and was dashed to pieces. The Culloo flew away, satisfied.

Poor Badger. There he lay, in a hundred pieces, except for his backbone which remained whole.

On the following day, along came Little Brother, crying bitterly, "Oh, my brother, why have you deserted me?"

At the sound of Little Brother's voice, Badger's backbone suddenly stood up all by itself and Badger's voice cried out:

"Ho, my leg come hither!" and the leg came and attached itself to the backbone. "Ho, my arm come hither!" cried the voice, and so it went on, Badger crying upon all the parts of his body until all the scattered bone and muscle and sinew and skin came together, and he was his old self again.

Little Brother clapped his hands with joy.

"That's a good trick," said Badger. "Too bad I can't do it again. Never mind, Little Brother, we can have plenty of fun without it."

So the two went on through the forest until they came to a hill and saw a huge stone. This, as it happened, was Koondao the booöin in his stone shape, but Badger had no idea of it.

"Let's have a race," cried Badger, and levering the stone from the earth, he sent it rolling down the hill.

Badger and his brother ran after it at top speed, shouting, "We can run faster than you!" They chased it to the bottom of the hill and raced past in triumph.

"We won, we won!" cried Little Brother, and sat down to recover his breath.

Badger was about to do the same when he heard a strange noise and looked around. There was the great stone coming straight at them.

"Run for your life, Little Brother!" cried Badger.

The stone thundered after them, up hills and down valleys, smashing rocks and trees in its path, gaining on the two Micmacs inch by inch. At the last moment, Badger thrust Little Brother to one side and allowed Koondao to strike him instead. The stone rolled over Badger, grinding him to powder, all of him this time, even his backbone. Then at last Koondao came to a halt, satisfied.

When all was still, Little Brother came and looked at the scattered bits of his brother and began to cry.

"The *teomul* will not work again," he sobbed. "I have lost my brother forever." But suddenly a voice thundered behind him.

"Koondao, you miserable stone, how dare you harm my people!" And there stood Glooscap, enlarged to an appalling size, so tall that his head touched the sky. In his fury the Great Chief set a light to the rock, and it burst into fire and burned down to black flakes. Then, returning to his normal size, Glooscap touched the flakes with his foot and they turned into flies.

"Little Brother," said the Great Chief sadly, "Badger was warned, but he would not listen. If he had not used up his charm to escape the Culloos, it would have protected him from Koondao."

Then, seeing the misery on Little Brother's face, he added, "However, Badger gave his life to save yours, so perhaps there is hope for him yet. I think we will give him one more chance." And, touching his magic belt, the Great Chief shouted:

"Ho, Badger's leg come hither" and "Ho, Badger's arm come hither," and so on, until Badger stood before them, his old self again, but somewhat thoughtful.

"That bit of fun was nearly my end," he remarked. "I hope I remember to be more careful in the future."

The Great Chief smiled and called down one of the black flies from the tree around which they were buzzing. Suddenly, Badger jumped, then he howled as the black fly bit him again.

"That will remind you!" said Glooscap, roaring with laughter. "Each spring the black flies will come to the forest to tell you that an act which causes pain to others will in the end cause pain to yourself."

And it is so to this day. The savage black flies still swarm through the eastern woodlands of Maine and the Maritime Provinces, reminding us of the Great Chief's words, as they reminded Badger long ago.

Once more, kespeadooksit—the story ends.

Glooscap and Winpe

In the Old Time of the Wabanaki, a wizard named Winpe ruled over the cold Northern Sea and had his lodge on a rocky island guarded by icebergs. Winpe was a powerful giant, cheerful but quick-tempered, who delighted in games and tests of magic.

Now when his messenger, Gray Gull, brought him tales of another great magician named Glooscap, who ruled over the land of the Wabanaki, Winpe at once sent a challenge. Glooscap returned word by Gray Gull that all his days were busy caring for his people and he had no time for games. Disappointed and angry, Winpe sent the lord of men and beasts this message: "Accept my challenge, Glooscap, or men will call you coward!"

The Great Chief said to Gray Gull in reply, "Tell your

master I know my people and they know me. I care not what fools call me."

When Winpe heard this, he smashed his fist against a huge rock and split it end to end, and the sound of his voice echoed around the icebergs.

"By all the gods of Sea and Sky, Glooscap shall compete with me before the moon grows full again!"

One evening soon afterwards, the Great Chief returned from hunting, and found his lodge empty. This was unusual, for Marten was always faithful, and Noogumee should at this hour be preparing his evening meal. Then Glooscap noticed that his dish of magic food lay overturned by the fire, as if Noogumee had been suddenly disturbed at her cooking.

Glooscap strode from his lodge to the edge of Blomidon and looked down. Far below, he saw a great canoe slide into the waters of Minas Basin. An Indian as tall as himself, but clothed all in furs, held his paddle high in mocking salute. It was Winpe the Wizard, and in the bottom of his canoe, bound and helpless, lay Noogumee and Marten.

Calling his two dogs, Day and Night, Glooscap started down the slope. Leaping ahead, the dogs dashed into the waves and swam after Winpe's canoe, but the wizard reached out and scooped the two dogs into his hands. He breathed on them with his arctic breath and they began to shrink. Once, twice, three times his breath passed over them, and the great dogs became as little puppies. Then Winpe set them in a wooden dish and floated them back to shore.

"Now, O Chief," he shouted triumphantly, "we have had our first contest. Follow if you can, and we will see who has the greater power!" And with one thrust of his paddle, he sent the canoe flying across Minas Basin.

Glooscap sprang into his own canoe and set off in furious pursuit. He was a mighty paddler and crossed Minas Basin before you could say Ableegumooch. Even so, when he reached the far shore, Winpe and his captives were out of sight. The Great Chief looked for the prow mark of Winpe's canoe and, finding it, followed the footmarks that led off into the forest. All that day and all the next, he raced along the trail, leaping fallen trees and tumbling brooks, knowing from the position of a twig or a strip of bark left secretly by Marten that he was on the right track.

On the third day the path opened into a clearing and before him stood a crooked old woman with live toads growing out of her hair.

"Kwah-ee, grandmother," cried Glooscap. "Have you seen Winpe the Wizard?"

"Yes, indeed," said she. "He passed this morning. Follow me and I'll lead you to him by a shorter way." And lifting her skirts, she ran like the wind. She ran so fast that Glooscap had difficulty keeping her in sight. He ran faster, and still faster, until—just as he caught up with her—she vanished! Then Glooscap knew he had been fooled. The toad woman had led him far off Winpe's trail.

However, Glooscap was not dismayed. Returning to the clearing, he found the trail again and followed it by moonlight all through the night. As the sun rose, he heard the roar of the sea and found himself at the edge of the Atlantic Ocean. But even the sea could not stop the Wabanaki hero.

"Bootup!" he shouted mightily, "Bootup, your Master has need of you!"

Out of the sea rolled the great whale with his white plume of pipesmoke streaming behind him. Glooscap leapt upon his back, saying, "Carry me to the Northern Sea, to the home of Winpe the Wizard."

As Bootup swam north, the ocean grew colder and colder, and great ice-cakes floated past. At last, Glooscap saw a black island loom up behind a dazzling ring of blue-white icebergs. Slipping between the guardian peaks, Bootup set his master ashore at the mouth of a river which cut its way under the rocks.

"This underground river leads to Winpe's lodge, Master," Bootup said, "but I am too wide to swim through. I shall take a nap here until your return."

Glooscap sprang off Bootup's back into the icy water, and as he waded into the darkness of the tunnel, the rock roof grew lower and lower, and the sides began to close in. Soon he had to walk sideways to keep from being scraped, and finally it was a struggle to squeeze through at all. Then, suddenly, he stumbled through into a wide cavern—and he and the wizard stood face to face!

The giant grinned broadly.

"Welcome, friend. Now we can have our contest."

"I came only to take my companions away," said Glooscap coldly, and Noogumee and Marten started forward joyfully. Just then there was the ominous sound of grinding rock, and looking back, Glooscap saw the rock wall close in behind him with a fearful crash. He too was a prisoner!

"Our contest will be in three parts," said Winpe calmly, "and when it is over, you and your friends may go in peace."

Glooscap now saw that it would be quicker in the end to agree.

"Very well," said he, "but let it be quick, for I have more important things to do."

Winpe, pointing to strings of ice-blue sapphires and shining pearls hung about the cave, said that Glooscap might have what he wished for his prize if he won.

"If I win," said Winpe, "I claim your amethyst beads."

Glooscap nodded agreement and the first test began.

Expanding his great chest, Winpe filled his lungs with the icy vapor of the Arctic and exhaled it in great blasts about the cave. Noogumee and Marten began to shake in the frosty air, but Glooscap did not even shiver. Winpe blew an even colder blast, and ice began to coat their bodies. By now, Noogumee and Marten lay stretched out as stiff as icicles.

"Your cave has grown warm," muttered Glooscap, his tongue moving with difficulty between his frozen teeth. "Can't you cool it?"

Winpe shrugged and smiled his defeat. Now it was Glooscap's turn.

The Great Chief arose, made a small fire, and touched

his magic belt. At once a great supply of firewood and oil appeared and fell upon the fire, and the flames shot up to the top of the cave. Marten and Noogumee, who had revived with the warmth, now wilted under the red-hot blasts of air from the fire. Choked by the fumes they fell back, once more unconscious. But Winpe sat in his place without moving. His beard was singed and great drops of sweat hissed as they rolled down his burning skin, yet he man-

aged to speak through parched lips.

"Don't you find it somewhat chilly in here, my friend?" he asked. "Put more wood on the fire."

Glooscap saw that his efforts were useless and let the fire die, and Noogumee and Marten came back to life again.

"We are even so far," cried Winpe. "Now for the final test!"

He brought forth two long sticks with webbing at the ends, and gave one of them to Glooscap together with a stuffed moosehide ball.

"This is a game I call *tokhonon*. As you see, I have set up two posts at each end of my cave. We must strike the ball back and forth, never touching it with our hands, and whoever first drives it between the other's goal posts, wins!"

Glooscap nodded his understanding, and the match began.

Ah, what a game that was! The two great heroes, each so tall and powerful, struck out with such force their sticks tore holes in the rock, and the whole cave trembled and cracked. Outside in the sea, Bootup woke with a start and heard with alarm the awesome rumbling. The black island heaved and shook, causing the waves to rise and sweep over Bootup's head.

For the space of three suns, while Noogumee and Marten watched breathlessly, the game continued without pause. Both players were by now nearly exhausted, yet neither had a single thought of giving in.

Suddenly Glooscap thought of the time that was passing. How were his people managing without him? What if Badger were up to some new tricks? The thought gave him fresh energy and, leaping high in the air, he struck the ball with such force it turned into a ball of fire and shot, burning, into Winpe's goal.

Winpe stepped back, his jaw falling with dismay.

Then, slowly, he summoned up a grin and came and slapped Glooscap on the shoulder.

"You are the winner," he said heartily. "It was a good game. Now choose your prize."

Glooscap looked at Winpe's strings of pearls and sapphires and shook his head. He held out his hand for Winpe's webbed stick.

"Give me the game," he said.

Now in his time, Glooscap had given many good gifts to his people—the forests, the streams, the fish and the animals—but no gift was cherished more than the game he brought back to them from Winpe's island, the game the Indians called *tokhonon,* the game the white man was one day to copy and call lacrosse.

And, with this last adventure, kespeadooksit—the stories end.